"I'm sure this is where they've taken Commander Kellie," Alex said.

"They're using her ... ic/mechanical jail experiment."

"So you're telling ... door than just steel and concrete?" ... asked Alex. "It sure looks like a normal building."

"Well, if I read the schematics right, behind these doors is a simulation of...an entirely different period in time. A very convincing one."

"Well, whatever it is, we have to get in there. Commander Kellie needs us," Paul insisted. Rapper nodded his agreement.

Phhhhhhsssssssss—pop!

"Door's open!" Alex announced.

As the three boys peeked in, their eyes opened wide.

Inside the drab, crumbling building was another world—just as Alex had anticipated. Deep, hunter-green leaves and tree trunks, some stunted, some magnificent, stretched a short way before breaking open to a wide, country meadow. The fresh smell of running water tickled their noses while bird chirps and animal squeaks rang in their ears. And was that a draft of...sulfur?

"Remember," Alex whispered, "it's just holograms and mechanics."

"*That* sure doesn't look like holograms and mechanics to me," Rapper admitted.

"Whoa! Look!" Paul exclaimed. Rapper and Alex followed Paul's pointing fingertip through the forest and past the open field beyond. There, on a distant, large hill it stood, dominating and wide—a black-bricked castle with at least five crooked turrets.

Alex gulped.

"Are you thinking what I'm thinking?" Rapper asked Paul.

"I bet I know just where we'll find Commander Kellie," Paul said. He thrust a clenched fist into the air and cried, "Let's go get us some shining armor, men! We're about to rescue our commander...as the first Superkid knights!"

Look for these other books in the *Commander Kellie and the Superkids*_{sm} Adventures Series!

*Commander Kellie and the Superkids*_{SM}

#11

The Knight-Time Rescue of Commander Kellie

Christopher P.N. Maselli

KENNETH
COPELAND
PUBLICATIONS

All scripture is from the following translations:

The Holy Bible, New International Version, © 1973, 1978, 1984 by the International Bible Society. Used by permission of Zondervan Publishing House.

International Children's Bible, New Century Version, © 1986, 1988 by Word Publishing, Dallas, Texas 75039. Used by permission.

*Commander Kellie and the Superkids*_{SM} is a registered servicemark of Heirborne_{TM}.

Based on the characters created by Kellie Copeland, Win Kutz, Susan Wehlacz and Loren Johnson.

The Knight-Time Rescue of Commander Kellie

ISBN 1-57562-874-0   30-0911

10 09 08 07 06 05   6 5 4 3 2 1

©2005 Eagle Mountain International Church, Inc. aka Kenneth Copeland Publications

Kenneth Copeland Publications
Fort Worth, Texas 76192-0001

For more information about Kenneth Copeland Ministries, call (800) 600-7395 or visit www.kcm.org.

**For Ryan Brockington,
Joel Davis and Stephen Glenn—
a.k.a. the "Superkid guys"—our
knights in shining armor.**

Contents

Hey Superkid!

You and I know monsters aren't real. But the devil doesn't want us to know that. He works overtime to convince us that maybe—just maybe—there's a big, ugly, hairy, bad-breathed beast underneath our beds. He doesn't want us to ever discover how to stand against his mind-games. But I'm here to tell you, I've met a monster head-on...and I've found what it takes to face it!

My name is Paul West and I'm a member of Superkid Academy. I'm in the Blue Squad with my friends Missy, Rapper, Valerie and Alex. Our leader, as you may know, is Commander Kellie. While Valerie and Missy were on another mission, Commander Kellie, Alex, Rapper and I just had an amazing adventure.

It began when the commander was mysteriously kidnapped right under our noses. I was supposed to watch her...and I let my guard down. When we found out where she was taken, it was out of this world—almost literally. And who was keeping her under lock and key? I'm telling you the truth: It was a monster! If it wasn't for the power of God's Word...well...

Have I stirred your interest? Then join me on an adventure into a place like no other on earth...a "world" unlike any you've ever imagined!

Paul

The Knight-Time Rescue of Commander Kellie

Paul didn't like it. The air was too still. The street was too quiet. The area was too enclosed. And his commander was out there alone.

From behind the corner of a concrete building, Paul watched...and waited. He glanced across the long corridor of buildings to the old, abandoned Jennings' Animation Studios. Twenty years ago, the successful founders moved uptown with the rest of the businesses. Their old building never sold. It probably never would. Neither would any of the other buildings within a 10-mile radius. This was the dead end of downtown. Even the undercity gangs had moved out.

That's why Commander Kellie suspected something was up. That's why Paul knew something wasn't right. From a dark corner of the animation studio building, Rapper nodded. Commander Kellie cautiously walked down the street. Paul could see her from the back—her shoulder-length, brown hair tumbled onto her commander's uniform. It was the same royal blue as the uniforms Paul and Rapper wore. As a commander should, she walked stately—not stiffly, but regal. Her walk came from inside her. It came from who she was.

Brushing his wavy, blond hair back with one hand, Paul bit his lip as he waited. At 14, he was the oldest Superkid in the Blue Squad—and perhaps because of his age, he was always considered the most adventurous. But that didn't mean Paul liked throwing caution to the wind. He raised his ComWatch to his mouth and spoke into the short-range communication device.

"We should abort—someone's going to get hurt!" he whispered. Across the way, brown-eyed Rapper pushed a button on his watch, bringing up Paul's image.

"Let's just keep a lookout," he responded, never taking his eyes off the street.

Commander Kellie spoke loud enough for her ComWatch to pick up her voice, but she didn't look into its micro-camera.

"Somebody sent us a call for help," she said. "I don't like this either. But if it's real, we need to be here. If it's not, I need you to be paying attention and ready for anything."

Paul shook his head. He knew Commander Kellie was right, but that didn't make it any easier. He hadn't felt good about the mission from the start. It had been only 24 hours earlier that the commander had received the simple, electronic note:

COMMANDER KELLIE:
NEED HELP.
COME TO ECHO BLVD, DWNTN, ALONE.
TOMORROW AFTERNOON.
WILL MEET YOU THERE.

Commander Kellie had decided to pursue the call for assistance—but with Paul and Rapper backing her up. If this was some sort of plot against her, she wanted to be ready.

Now they were here, along the short stretch of Echo Boulevard. Rapper stood at one end, hidden. Paul was concealed at the other end and Commander Kellie patrolled the middle, waiting for whoever wrote the message to arrive. Two side streets intersected Echo Boulevard, but provided little cover for the Superkids, so they remained at the far stretches.

"There's going to be trouble. I just know you're going to get caught or something," Paul said into his ComWatch, immediately wishing he could take it back.

"Paul, don't say that," Commander Kellie said, still walking forward and eyeing the buildings. "Remember, the words you speak are process starters."

"I don't want you to get into a bad situation," Paul assured his commander.

"Then don't say things like that," Commander Kellie ordered. "Words are powerful—even God never does anything without saying it first."

Paul nodded. He bent his fingers around the cold, gritty edge of the building as he watched. The only sound was an occasional, echoing tap from Commander Kellie's boot.

"Paul?" Paul glanced down at his ComWatch. It was Commander Kellie. She still wasn't looking in her watch, but he could hear her.

"Yes?" he asked.

"Thank you for caring," was all she said—but the words spoke volumes to the Superkid. Paul *did* care for his commander. She was his leader through mission after tough mission. One mission in particular he could still remember as though it were only the week prior. In reality, though, it had been three years ago....

Each member of the Blue Squad was still getting used to working as a team—Paul, Missy, Rapper, Valerie and Alex.

Commander Kellie had led them on a mission to thwart a secret NME plan. NME—*Notoriously Malicious Enterprises*—was an organization committed to making "big bucks" on its way to stopping the gospel. The Superkids discovered NME had secretly planted explosives in the basement level of a convention hall—and the Superkids had less than six hours to find and disarm all of them. Of course, the real test had been accomplishing their task undercover—the entrances had all been manned by NME guards.

To make a long story short, when Commander Kellie and the Superkids had arrived, the lone entrance they found into the basement was a tiny window that only the kids could slide through. It was at that moment Commander Kellie had said the words for the first time: "Paul, you're in charge." The Superkid's heart leapt with courage. His commander trusted him—immensely. Paul led the Superkids to saving the day, even though no one in the world ever knew about it. But retrieving and disarming the bombs wasn't what had encouraged Paul. It was knowing his commander believed in him.

Then again, in some ways it was more than that. Commander Kellie had also become Paul's friend. He could trust her anytime, in any situation. He knew she wouldn't lead him the wrong way. And he knew she cared. That's why her correction—even now—didn't hurt. He knew she was helping him become a better person.

Clink!

"Did you hear something?" 12-year-old Rapper asked.

Paul listened. "Yeah," he responded, whispering into his ComWatch.

Like a slow crab, a chill crawled down Paul's spine. Something was about to happen. He knew it.

Paul looked down at his watch. He could see Rapper gazing forward. "Look, I really think we ought to—"

Rapper looked at Paul through the ComWatch. "Quit looking into your ComWatch!" he whispered. "Keep your eyes on—"

Whoossshhhh...

Paul and Rapper looked up with a start.

Commander Kellie was gone.

Completely gone.

Paul took immediate charge. "Let's go!" he shouted into his watch. Rapper didn't need any convincing. He was already headed to the center of the street.

Paul raced forward, slapping his ComWatch and shouting for his commander. "Commander Kellie! Commander Kellie!!!" She didn't respond.

Rapper met Paul in the center of the street and they glanced down the adjoining avenues.

"There!" Rapper shouted, pointing down Henson Drive. Paul whirled around to catch a glimpse of a wide shadow. The Superkids raced to Henson and stopped in their tracks when they arrived. The shadow belonged to a quickly approaching black hovercraft. There were no markings on it, but it didn't take a Warren Technologies scientist to know it wasn't friendly.

Paul and Rapper turned around as the ship banked to the right and steadied itself behind them.

Pzzzzzowwww!

Paul and Rapper leapt forward as a laser blast smashed the ground by their feet.

"Let's get out of here!" Rapper shouted the obvious.

Still, Paul protested, "Not without Commander Kellie!"

"She's already gone!" Rapper yelled.

Pzzzzzowwww! Another blast exploded beside Paul. He jumped aside and glanced back at the ship. The windows were dark. He knew they had Commander Kellie. But there was nothing he could do about it.

"Over here!" Rapper cried as he slid into the entranceway of an abandoned building. Paul followed. The ship angled up and took off, leaving a trail of dirty, black smoke in its wake.

Paul stepped out and watched it leave.

"They were just trying to scare us," he noted as Rapper joined his side. "They only wanted the commander."

"It worked," Rapper observed.

Paul's heart was beating fast. He tapped his ComWatch again.

"Commander Kellie!"

No response.

"I'm sorry," Paul whispered into his watch.

✪   ✪   ✪

"It *is* my fault!" Paul argued. "Commander Kellie was caught because of *my* words! I said she'd get caught and it happened just like I said! Proverbs 6:2—she was 'snared by my words.' End of story. Now it's up to me to get her back!"

The Superkid Academy Control Room was nearly empty, except for a few young workers performing routine maintenance.

"Well, I'm in," Rapper assured his friend, punching his shoulder. "I don't care how it happened—I just want to get her back."

"Except we have no *clue* as to where to start. Not to mention that Alex is gone and Missy and Valerie are on another mission."

"Actually, I know exactly where to start!" said a voice from behind.

Paul and Rapper jumped in surprise.

"Alex!" Rapper cried. Alex was smiling wide, standing in his royal-blue Superkid uniform. A few years younger than Paul, Alex had dark skin, short, black hair and brown eyes. He was a bit shorter, too, but Paul kept expecting him to have a growth spurt any day that would shoot him up taller than them all. Paul respected Alex a great deal for his technological know-how. He could even run circles around most adults.

Paul and Rapper gave their friend a hug. Then Paul asked, "Where'd you come from?!"

"I've been on a mission myself," Alex answered. He looked around. "Where's Commander Kellie?"

Paul looked at Rapper. "That's the bad news," he admitted. "We left yesterday to answer a call for help and—"

Alex's mouth dropped. "They got her?! Already?!"

"You know who took her?" Paul pressed.

Alex shook his head. "No, I don't. But I think I know where to find her."

"You do?!" Paul shouted.

"I do," Alex answered. "The mission the Lord sent me on led me to *this*."

A long, beige cylinder of paper was rolled up in Alex's dark fists. Paul and Rapper looked at it in wonderment. Alex moved over to the long, purplish, Superkid mission table at the east corner of the control room. He set the cylinder down and unrolled it.

"It looks old," Rapper observed. Paul nodded.

The cylinder revealed a crude map within its coils. Certain spots were labeled: STABLES, CAVE, DARK CASTLE, LAKE, WELL 1, WELL 2, VILLAGE, DUNGEON A, O.S. LAIR and more. At the top of the map was some sort of bar code:

And running down the side were the words, "2236 Roland Drive."

"Roland Drive?" Rapper questioned. "That's near where Commander Kellie was caught."

"Then they didn't take her far," Alex noted.

Paul pointed to a series of wavy lines on the map. "What are these?"

Alex explained that he believed the map was for a sophisticated, interactive, holographic environment actually within whatever building was located at 2236 Roland Drive.

"What do you mean, 'interactive, holographic environment?'" Paul wondered.

"I mean," Alex said, "someone has combined mechanics and holograms to create a small world within the confines of four walls. In essence, you could think you're walking several miles within this world and you'll have only gone a couple of feet."

Paul looked at Rapper. Rapper looked at Paul.

Alex explained, "In other words, I think someone created a holographic world set in medieval times...*inside* the building."

"What? You mean it's like a giant video game?" Rapper asked.

"More like a time machine," Alex answered. "Once you enter the building, you'll *feel* like you've entered another time period."

"So why was Commander Kellie taken there?"

"We won't know unless we go," Alex replied.

Paul nodded. "Then, let's go!"

A full day has passed and I haven't had a good look at my captors. I don't know what they want from me. They haven't hurt me. They haven't asked any questions. But they <u>did</u> kidnap me.

When I awoke, I found myself in these tight, damp quarters. The room is basically empty except for a few trinkets that appear to be centuries old. I found an old pen, a bottle of ink and some paper among the trinkets, so I will record my thoughts.

A smell like rotten eggs is heavy in the air. The room is very tall and four small, square openings are in the wall opposite the door. They're near the ceiling and provide fresh air and light for writing. When I look up, I can see clouds and treetops. The smell of fresh water occasionally blows in.

I wonder if this is how the Apostle Paul felt when he was in jail writing letters to the churches. I don't know if I am here because of my stand for the Word, but I imagine so. The words of the Apostle Paul in Ephesians 6:19-20 come to mind: "Pray also for me, that whenever I open my mouth, words may be given me so that I will fearlessly make known the mystery of the gospel, for which I am an ambassador in chains. Pray that I may declare it fearlessly, as I should."

Lord, I echo his prayer.

Kellie

✪ ✪ ✪

The three Superkids stood at the heart of old downtown. It wasn't a pretty place, even in the daytime. The buildings were large, deteriorating and abandoned like sunken ships...Titanics filled with stale air instead of water.

The building that loomed before them was the largest of them all: 2236 Roland Drive, a huge arena that looked as vacant as the rest. Nonetheless, the buzzing coming from behind its boarded windows hinted that there was a surprise wrapped up inside.

"I'm sure this is where they've taken Commander Kellie," Alex said, nodding. "And the more I look at this map, the more I think they've created some kind of holographic/mechanical jail experiment."

"The question is who are *'they?'* " Paul added.

Alex walked up to the front door and pushed on it. The massive door wouldn't budge. Alex spied a metal box adjacent to the door. "It's electronically sealed," he announced, "but I think I can break the seal with a bit of rewiring."

"Do it," Paul ordered. Alex nodded and pulled out a set of pocket tools. He began to work.

"So you're telling us that there's more behind this door than just steel and concrete?" Rapper asked Alex. "It sure looks like a normal building."

"Yep, there's a whole world inside."

"So this is like a time machine?" Paul pressed, slapping the brick with his hand.

"No," Alex corrected, "just a *simulation* of another time. But all indications are that it'll be a very convincing one."

"Well, whatever it is, we have to get in there. Commander

Kellie needs us," Paul insisted. Rapper nodded his agreement.

Phhhhhhsssssss—pop!

"Door's open!" Alex announced.

"Let's go!" cried Paul, climbing the steps to the building.

"No—wait!" Alex responded. "We can't just go in."

"Why not?"

"We'll stick out like sore thumbs in these uniforms. We need to dress as the simulation dictates."

"So what kind of dress does 'the simulation dictate'?" Rapper asked Alex.

"Let's have a look so we know for sure," Alex answered, pushing the door aside.

As the three boys peeked in, their eyes opened wide.

Inside the drab, crumbling building *was* another world—just as Alex had anticipated. Deep, hunter-green leaves and tree trunks, some stunted, some magnificent, stretched a short way before breaking open to a wide, country meadow. The fresh smell of running water tickled their noses while bird chirps and animal squeaks rang in their ears. And was that a draft of...sulfur?

"Remember," Alex whispered, "it's just holograms and mechanics."

"That sure doesn't look like holograms and mechanics to me," Rapper admitted.

A squirrel ran up to the door's threshold and vanished when it hit the perimeter to the real world. Rapper looked at Alex and nodded his acceptance of what he had said.

"Whoa! Look!" Paul exclaimed. Rapper and Alex followed Paul's pointing fingertip through the forest and past the open field beyond. There, on a distant, large hill it stood, dominating and wide—a black-bricked castle with at least five crooked turrets.

Alex gulped.

"Are you thinking what I'm thinking?" Rapper asked Paul.

Paul nodded. "I bet I know just where we'll find Commander Kellie."

"And I know just what we'll have to wear to blend in," Rapper concluded.

Paul thrust a clenched fist into the air and cried, "Let's go get us some shining armor, men! We're about to rescue our commander...as the first Superkid knights!"

✪ ✪ ✪

"I feel a little ridiculous in this," Paul noted as he clanked up the steps of 2236 Roland Drive with Rapper and Alex. Each Superkid was dressed in a full suit of armor. From their feet to their legs, to their waists, around their torso and over their arms, each young man looked like he had just stepped out of a storybook tale of King Arthur's court. The metal glistened in the afternoon sun. Their breastplates each had a simple cross etched on them—making the suits all the more appropriate, Paul thought. A simple, but worthy, sword was at Paul's side— the one piece of the costume that *was* genuine—and he cradled his helmet in the crook of his elbow. A blue feather stemmed from the back of the helmet.

"Are you kiddin'?" Rapper questioned. "We look like we're ready for anything!" He slapped the helmet he held and it rang with a hollow thump.

"I'm just glad the costume shop had real, metal suits," Alex noted, "or these wouldn't do us much good inside." The costume shop suits weren't extremely tough, but they were convincing. Plus, they had the benefits of modern technology that allowed for fairly easy movement.

Paul made a fist and looked at his hand inside the tight glove. A metal covering shaped like a loose fist hooded his hand.

Sliding a supply pack over his shoulder, Alex opened the heavy door to the building again and they looked inside. It was just as they had left it: plenty of greenery, the echoes of critters, the sweet smells of running water and a black castle in the distance. Paul glanced at Rapper and Alex.

"You're in charge," Rapper said to Paul, unenthusiastically. Paul's forehead wrinkled. It sounded so much better when Commander Kellie said it.

Slowly, Paul stepped forward and entered the building. A gathering of leaves crunched beneath his first footstep. He reached down and picked up a leaf. As he squeezed, it crumbled in his hand. He peeked back at Alex.

"How come it seems so real if this is just a hologram?" he wondered.

Alex's eyes lit up. "They're called Textured Holograms. They actually look, feel and act like the real thing—but they're not. Some of them have mechanics under the surface, some don't. Until now, they've only been possible in theory...apparently someone has proven that theory right."

"I'm not looking forward to finding out who," Paul said beneath his breath. He took another step forward, his armor clanking. He could hear Rapper and Alex following in his footsteps.

It was absolutely believable—like they had just entered a completely different country...or time period...or world. A breeze of cool air brushed Paul's cheek. If he hadn't just walked through a door, he wouldn't have believed he was inside a building. Above, the tall trees broke way to a deep, blue sky and a bright, shining sun. A bird in a nearby branch caught Paul's eye as it sang hello to the new visitors. And beyond—far in the distance—was the castle they had noticed earlier.

"Uh-oh."

Paul closed his eyes. He didn't like hearing those words uttered—especially at the beginning of a mission. Slowly, he turned around, his armor clinking with each movement.

Alex was facing the direction they had just come from. Paul heard him say, "We lost the door."

Rapper leaned forward and felt the tree behind them. "How could we lose the door?" he asked.

"It makes sense, actually," Alex reasoned. "The environment is automatically adjusting to our presence—and will as long as we're here. The holo-transmitters are forging the environment around us."

"Yo—English, Alex," Rapper said.

"We're stuck in here," Alex said plainly.

Paul huffed.

"I knew we should have brought our ComWatches," Rapper pointed out. But Alex shook his head.

"No—we have to completely blend in with the simulation. That means no modern-day technology, or we'll give ourselves away."

"We're wearing sneakers under our armor," Rapper noted.

Alex nodded. "But sneakers don't beep and warble."

Paul walked to a river flowing nearby and touched the water. It was so believably real. It was cool. It was wet. And Alex was telling them this was just a holographic experience?

A sudden horse's whinny took Paul by surprise. He whirled

around, wrapping a hand around the hilt of his sword.

The horse's gallop echoed through the trees, making the single, approaching animal sound like a dozen. Then suddenly, the galloping stopped. The horse whinnied.

"Who goes there?" a deep voice shouted through the wood. The horse whinnied again. "Show thyself bold!"

Paul looked at his companions and wondered what to do. But before he had time to decide, a chestnut horse with a slick coat came into view. Atop the horse, a tall man in burgundy, blue and dark-green clothes pulled back on the reins. The horse obediently stopped. The man's thick, red beard covered his neck. He looked down his nose as he said, "Ah! Fair gents! Be thou deaf, or timid?"

The Superkids remained silent. Paul knew the others were thinking what he was thinking: *Who is this guy?* Paul hadn't expected to meet any people.

Paul leaned in to Rapper and whispered, "You think he wants us to greet him?"

Rapper nodded. Then he stepped forward and began tapping a beat on his armored chest.

"Yo there, rad, my name is Rapper R," he rapped, "Comin' straight at ya with the love of the Lor—"

Alex jumped forward and grabbed Rapper's hands in midbeat. He looked at his friend. "B-L-E-N-D," he spelled.

Paul realized what Alex was saying—the man on the horse was part of the simulation. Another hologram. Paul stepped forward himself and nodded. He put forth his best "knight" voice, speaking like he'd seen them do in the movies.

"Greetings, friend," Paul said. "I'm Sir Paul West of Sawyer. This is Sir Robert and Sir Alex. We come from afar."

"*Sir?*" the horseman questioned. "Thou art knights? Pardon my lips, but thou art a bit youthful for knighthood."

"Not so, my good man," Paul corrected. "The Holy Scriptures saith, 'The glory of young men is their strength.'"

The man's eyebrows hopped up. "Holy Scriptures?"

"Verily," Paul said, "they tell of Christ Jesus, the Son of the Living God." Paul was beginning to enjoy talking like a knight. He reached into a crook of his armor to pull out a small Bible he brought along when suddenly the man said, "I have not heard of such." He pulled on his beard. Paul blinked in surprise.

"I thought you said they built this place historically accurate," Paul whispered to Alex.

Alex whispered back, "Looks like someone left the Word out—probably on purpose."

"Who is this bard who speaks so softly?" the man asked, pointing at Alex.

Alex smiled when he realized he was being addressed. "I, uh, I art Sir Alex Taylor and I beseech thou noble one, oh noble one."

Rapper nudged Alex in the side, clanking his elbow against Alex's breastplate. "Way to B-L-E-N-D, oh noble one," he kidded.

Paul tucked his Bible back into his armor. He was still thinking about what Alex had said a moment earlier. Someone had created a perfect simulation...except it was a world *without* the Word. *A world without God's Word.* Paul realized it wasn't such a perfect simulation after all.

"Friend," Paul addressed the man. "Thou art...?"

"Andrew," the man responded, smiling, "from o'er yon bend, in the hollow."

"Andrew," Paul said warmly. "My men and I seek a fair

maiden named Kellie. She hath been taken...and we determine to find her."

Patting his horse's neck, Andrew looked down into the brush thoughtfully.

"What dost thou know?" Paul pressed.

"Many a fair lady and gentleman have disappeared over time, gents," he said softly. "'Tis the way of Old Scratch. He taketh as he wishes and he destroyeth his opponent. None can withstand his fury."

Paul felt a sudden burning within his spirit. "Where is this 'Scratch'? He shall meet his match today!"

"Thou?!?" Andrew snickered. "And what troops shall join thee? No one stands against Old Scratch."

Paul held Andrew's eye.

"Thou dost have a fire within," Andrew admitted. "But there be no reasoning with Scratch. Nor canst thou prepare for battle in want of victuals and horses. Lodge with me this night. I will tell thee of Scratch—and thou mayest decide thy destiny thereafter."

Paul looked at Rapper and Alex.

"Hey," Rapper offered, "let's find out everything we can. Maybe we can get some clues about how to rescue Commander Kellie."

"I hast to agreeth," Alex said.

"Very well," Paul announced. "We accept thy hospitality."

"Splendid!" Andrew grabbed the reigns of his horse. Then, with a glance over his shoulder toward the dominating silhouette of the castle in the distance, he added, "Methinks thou wilt have need of it!"

3
Scratch

After many hours, food has finally been delivered. The opening of the door surprised me—so much so that I wasn't ready to grab the door before it closed. I only saw the reddish color of a man's hand as a crude tray holding a chicken leg and a potato was shoved into the room.

The draft that came in when the door was opened almost bowled me over. It's not rotten eggs as I first suspected, but sulfur, I believe. _Why_ there is such a strong smell of sulfur here, I don't know.

The longer I am here, the more I wonder the reason for being here. And then I begin to wonder where "here" is. I've been praying for these things to come to light. And I've also been praying for my Superkids. They've been on my mind a lot suddenly—especially Paul, Rapper and Alex. The Holy Spirit has shown me that something is up. Perhaps they are trying to find me. I just pray they have some idea as to where I am.

Father God, as the apostle in chains wrote in Ephesians 1:18, "may the eyes of our understanding be enlightened."

Kellie

✪ ✪ ✪

Andrew bit into a juicy slab of lamb that was skewered by a piece of metal he used like a utensil. The three Superkids sat around their new friend's wooden table and ate heartily with him. It took a bit of explaining as to why they wouldn't eat the food or drink the liquid he had offered. Alex said something about them all being on a special "knight diet." Andrew protested at first, but Alex persisted. The real reason, Alex explained to Paul, was that the holographic food and water wouldn't amount to anything in their stomachs, even though it might taste great going down. Paul didn't understand the physics of it at all, but that was OK. At least someone did. Instead, the Superkids drank water from their canteens and ate concentrated rations—regular Academy fare for emergency situations. The thick, brown bars didn't look too good, but they filled the stomach well.

Before dinner, Paul, Rapper and Alex had removed their suits of armor. They left them out at the barn, crumpled together in a corner. Now they wore tan shirts, jeans and athletic shoes. Andrew was quite fascinated by the jeans and shoes. For a moment, Alex was concerned they'd blown their cover, but Paul explained to Andrew that sneakers were quite popular where they came from, and Andrew accepted it.

After a bit of small talk, Paul brought the discussion back around to their reason for visiting. "So, dost thou know where our fair maiden is jailed?" he asked, still working on his medieval times voice.

"If she still lives," Andrew began, "she is surely kept at the dark castle."

"The dark castle?" Paul asked. He put down his ration. "'Twas that the abode we saw in the distance when we met thee?"

"Most certainly," Andrew replied.

Rapper chimed in. "That should be easy enough to reach. It was just on top of the hill."

"Aye, straight as the crow flieth," Andrew agreed, "but a path few adventurers dare take. Verily thou shalt be seen and Scratch shall be alerted to thy presence. Of a truth, better, 'tis said, to travel far toward the setting sun, then double back over the cliffs. But, 'tis rumored, the way is most treacherous— daunting to even the stoutest knight."

"I don't mind confronting Scratch face to face," Paul pointed out. "He needs a good wake-up call. What kind of man secretly kidnaps a maiden and carries her off to his kingdom, anyway?"

Andrew stopped chewing his bite of lamb. He stared at Paul and held his eyes steadily. Then he chuckled and stared at Paul again.

"Thinkest thou this, sir knight?" Andrew asked, his red beard shifting. "Thinkest thou Scratch a mere man?"

Alex's dark eyebrows bumped up onto his forehead. "What? Thou meaneth he's not a man-eth?"

"Sirs," Andrew addressed, "Scratch is a *dragon.*"

Rapper squinted, a bite of rations puckered in the side of his cheek. "You mean like a lizard-scaled, saber-clawed, cat-eyed, fire-breathing dragon?"

"And winged as well," Andrew said with a wink.

"No way," Rapper whispered.

Paul felt his temperature rise. "But dragons aren't real. They don't exist," he argued.

"Mayhap from whence thou comest," Andrew said, "but of a truth, they live."

The Superkids were silent as Andrew explained.

"As I said unto thee, Scratch ruleth our land as he pleases. Should he want, he taketh. For that he hath no want, he destroyeth. Shouldst thou seek thy fair maiden, it is through Scratch thou must go."

"Are you telling me we'll have to fight a dragon?" Paul questioned.

"Aye," Andrew said pushing away his plate. "And thou must win."

Paul glanced down at his rations. He wasn't hungry anymore.

$$\bigstar \quad \bigstar \quad \bigstar$$

"It can't be that bad," Paul said to Rapper and Alex. He set a small stack of wood in an iron stove.

For the night, Andrew lent the Superkids blankets and set up beds of hay for them in the stables. Past missions had provided worse conditions, so none of them seemed to mind much. Besides, their thoughts were still focused on that night's dinner topic.

"After all," Paul reasoned, "dragons are nothing but works of fiction."

"That may be true," Alex offered, "but remember, we're in a holographic world. Someone sure took the time to create this as real as possible. But we've already found out they left out a portion of history—God's Word. Now it looks like they've decided to create a little history of their own. They've added a dragon."

"It's probably the size of a Chihuahua or something," said Rapper, lightly.

"Right," Paul said. "A Chihuahua that holds the entire holoworld captive in the grasp of its paws."

Rapper and Alex chuckled, though Paul thought they sounded more nervous than amused.

Paul fumbled along the side of the iron stove and found a small lever. He turned it clockwise. The three boys watched as two iron gears inside scraped each other and created their own small fireworks of sparks.

"Check it out!" Rapper exclaimed.

One of the sparks hit a piece of kindling just right and started a small curl of yellow flame. Paul closed the stove and sat back, watching and staring as the flame turned into a raging fire.

Rapper was setting out his blanket on one of the haystacks when Paul's solemn demeanor caught his eye. He reached forward and shoved his friend, but Paul responded with a sour face.

"Yo, what's up?" Rapper questioned. Alex started working with his own blanket.

Paul shrugged. "That passage in James keeps coming to mind," he said, still staring ahead. "It says that a tiny spark can set a forest on fire. And the tongue is also a fire...which can destroy everything around it. In Matthew 12:36 Jesus said we'll each have to give account for every careless word we've spoken. My tongue started a fire that got Commander Kellie caught. And now we may have to fight a dragon. Even if it isn't real, I'm sure it'll act like it. By my simple, careless words, I've set in motion a path that could destroy us all."

"Yo!" Rapper interrupted. "Let's stop the confessing while you're ahead!"

Paul shook his head. He knew how it worked. The devil tries hard to plant words into your mind so you'll speak them out of your mouth and they'll drop into your spirit. It's plain and simple. But Paul wasn't supposed to let that happen. He wasn't supposed to listen to the fear the devil had thrown at him. He wasn't supposed to speak it out. But he had...and even now Paul's own words were working to hurt his commander, his best friends and himself.

"James 3:8 says no man can tame his tongue," Paul remembered sadly.

Alex sat up on his blanket. "Yeah," he agreed, "that's true that no *man* can tame the tongue. But God can tame our tongues with spiritual power. John 6:63 says the words God speaks are spirit. When we speak His words, they'll be backed by His power. As we continue to put His Word in our hearts, it'll come out of our mouths. And our tongues will be tamed."

"That's easier said than done," Paul protested.

Rapper tossed Paul the pocket Bible they had brought along with them. "That's just it," he said to his friend. "It must be said to be done."

The room fell silent except for the chirping of crickets and the occasional whinny of a horse. After about half an hour, Rapper and Alex leaned back and tucked themselves under their blankets.

Paul stayed up for a while though, and kept staring into the fire. As it danced in the stove, every flame seemed to remind him of the position in which he'd placed his friends.

Paul sniffed as the strong smell of hay and horses filled his nostrils. The air grew cooler and the fire eventually grew dimmer. But before it went out, Paul whispered a prayer. He knew they were in a holographic environment that had left God's Word out of its history. But that didn't mean God's Word wouldn't work. On the contrary, it was the only real thing there.

"I'm making a decision," Paul said, looking up to heaven. Through thin openings in the roof, he could see a couple of stars twinkle. "I'm making a decision to take control of my tongue. Father God, I'm sorry for every word I've spoken contrary to Your Word. I know that my mouth will speak whatever is in my heart. Luke 6:45 says it. So I'm going to start filling my mouth with Your Word. And I know when I speak it, Your Word will do what You want it to do."

The room remained silent and Paul's eyelids grew heavy. He lay back on the hay and pulled the woven blanket up to his chin. He, Rapper and Alex had a big day ahead of them. It was one he wanted to be ready for. He knew trouble was out there and he was about to face it....

✪   ✪   ✪

All six eyes popped open when they heard the sound in the full of the night. Shadows covered much of the stable around them, cast by beams and horses and the Superkids themselves. The chill of the air forced goose bumps to pop up on their skin.

Though they all awakened, no one moved. The sound was still there...all around them. It was like a slow rushing of air...a settling of electric power...the brush of a gigantic bird's wings.

Paul realized it was coming from above—above the stable. Something was out there moving through the air. It was something big—something evil.

Paul pulled the rough blanket tightly around his neck. No one said a word. Words weren't necessary. They knew what it was. They knew *who* it was. And Paul began to wonder if their presence in the new world was still a secret.

The Lord awakened me only minutes ago to pray for Paul. It's frustrating being imprisoned and not being able to be there for him. On the other hand, it's comforting to know that through prayer, I can reach further than I ever could on my own.

I confess 2 Timothy 1:7 over him now: "God did not give Paul a spirit of fear, but a spirit of power and love and self-discipline."

As I've begun, the Spirit has shown me that Paul, Rapper and Alex are looking for me. But I do not yet know how close...or how far away...they may be.

As the Scripture says in 1 Peter 5:8, the devil is on the prowl like a roaring lion, looking for someone to devour. But we will resist him. We will stand firm in our faith.

Kellie

✪   ✪   ✪

Unlike Rapper and Alex, Paul couldn't fall back to sleep. From the chilling moment he knew Scratch had flown over the stable, it was impossible for him to sleep another wink. Even before the dragon flew overhead, Paul dreamed more than once about their inevitable encounter. Each time in his dreams, the dragon appeared suddenly—surprisingly—and came diving down upon the unsuspecting Superkid knights.

Paul was now up and out in front of Andrew's house. He had washed up and put on his full suit of armor. He didn't quite feel used to it yet; the metal costume was awkward. Andrew had already left, off to visit relatives in the nearby village of Trenton.

Sffft! Paul slid his sword out of its brown, leather scabbard at his waist. The full weapon was over three feet long. It was made of fully tempered, high-carbon spring steel extending from a covered leather handle. It was no imitation—it was firm and authentic. When he tapped it against his armor, it had a quick and soft ringing sound. Paul swung the sword in front of him, slicing the air. It was heavy, but if he needed to, he imagined he could use it with only one hand. He sliced the air again.

Leaping forward, Paul cut the air one, two, three more times. He imagined he was sword-fighting with another brave knight. Left! Right! Left again! Paul would show him!

After zipping about Andrew's yard for half an hour, Paul took a break when he heard laughter behind him. Rapper stood there, dressed in his armor, too, with a wide smile on his face.

"Rad, that's great!" he exclaimed. "You can slice air like no other knight I've ever seen! If a tornado ever comes against me, I'm giving you a call!" Rapper laughed aloud again.

Paul stood still as Rapper approached him and pulled out his own sword. "Let me give you a few pointers," he said, still smiling.

Paul nodded. Rapper had spent some of his younger years as a part of an undercity gang. During that time—though he wasn't proud of it—he had learned to use hand weapons rather well. Paul imagined a sword was just a step away for the Superkid.

First, Rapper showed Paul how to properly grip the sword and how to stand.

"I didn't know there was so much technique to it," Paul admitted.

"There's not if you're just slicing air," Rapper responded. "But we may have to take the fire out of a dragon—not quite like battling the wind."

Rapper took a step back and dropped down his face plate. Paul followed his lead and did the same. Rapper's voice echoed from inside his suit as he instructed Paul.

"Now come at me with your sword and watch how I defend myself."

Paul nodded. He moved forward swinging and, with the new grip, actually found it easier to wield the sword than before.

Clang! Clang! Bang! Rapper blocked every shot.

"Now I'm going to come at you," Rapper said. He slid to the side and came at Paul quickly. Paul tried to block Rapper's blow—and did...the first time. The second whirl landed squarely on Paul's chest. He was immediately thankful for the armor.

On and on it went. For nearly a full hour, Paul listened to Rapper's pointers, tried new moves and kept getting hit in the chest. Finally, after a knock to the ground, Paul was exhausted.

"OK, I give up!" Paul shouted through his face plate. Rapper laughed. Paul's friend put away his sword and helped him up.

Paul and Rapper raised their face plates.

"That's harder than I thought," Paul said.

Rapper chuckled. "Took me four years to get that good. And actually, I'm not that great."

"What does that say about *my* sword-swinging?" Paul wondered aloud.

"You just need a little more time and patience."

"I'm about out of both," Paul said softly. He put his sword back at his side.

Rapper sat down on a large, nearby rock. "Just keep remembering that it's just fake," he consoled. "This whole place is imaginary. When it comes down to it, it's nothing more than holograms and mechanics."

"But why does there have to be a dragon?" Paul asked.

Rapper raised his eyebrows.

"When I was a little kid," Paul continued, "one night I stayed up at the orphanage and watched this movie. I was 'Mr. Big Rebel,' you know. Anyway, the whole thing was about this larger-than-life dragon that would swoop down at night and attack people. It creeped me out and gave me nightmares for a year straight."

"Rad, that's bad."

"Tell me about it. Want to know what's worse?"

Rapper nodded.

"What's worse is that I had one of those nightmares again last night. It's been nearly seven years since I've dreamed about that dragon. Maybe eight."

"Thank God, there's a difference now," said Rapper.

"What's that? That I finally might have to actually meet him face to face?"

"Well, that...but more importantly, now you have God's Word."

✪ ✪ ✪

While Alex strapped on his armor and Rapper closed up their camp in the stables, Paul spent some time alone with God. He read some scriptures and prayed. Then he read more scriptures and prayed some more. Paul knew his spirit man had to be ready for battle too.

Finally dressed in their full suits of armor, the three sat down to eat some rations before departing. As they took a few bites, Alex unrolled the map in front of them. He pointed to the castle at the center.

"So I had this idea," Alex explained. "Why not just locate the central processing unit to this place and shut it down? The simulation will end and we can rescue Commander Kellie with no problems."

"But..." Rapper coaxed.

"But," Alex continued, "I only have a theory as to where the CPU is located."

"And that is..." Rapper coaxed again.

Alex tapped on the map. "In the center of the simulation. Right in the middle of the dark castle somewhere."

"Well, good," Paul said with a nod. "That's where we're going."

Alex placed his finger near the top of the map, right under the bar code. "Best I can tell, this is where we are." He pulled his finger down through a long, wooded cove. "We'll have to go through here, which is a long way, but it's a direct route to the castle." He moved his finger to the left. "This looks like a village, even though it's not marked. Maybe it's Trenton. Anyway, it's far enough away that we shouldn't even have to go through it."

The rest of the route appeared rather direct to Paul. The

simplicity of it pleased him. Andrew had warned them that going directly to the castle could be dangerous. Scratch might see them, spoiling their surprise. But Paul felt ready. At this point, he preferred facing the dragon head-on anyway. During the night he had felt a bit edgy, but upon further contemplation, what was there to fear? The beast was nothing but light-trickery and mechanics. Besides, Andrew said the indirect route to the west was treacherous—and surely it would take more time...time they didn't want to waste.

"Let's go," Paul ordered.

✪ ✪ ✪

A morning and afternoon of trotting on horseback brought the Superkids closer to their destination, though they felt as though they still had light years to go. As the evening sun began to set on the exhausted Superkids, Paul decided it was time for them to rest for the night.

Andrew had kindly lent the three adventurers some horses, which Alex led to a nearby lake he had found. After a hearty drink, the horses, which they nicknamed Trigger, Silver and Mr. Ed, were tied to two trees. Rapper broke out the rectangular, brown rations and Paul searched for some good wood for their camp.

Two armfuls of logs and twigs were just what Paul wanted and he dropped them within a circle of rocks on a cleared mound of dirt. The wood burned hot and Alex even roasted his ration. He said it had the aftertaste of burnt s'mores.

"Mmm, a delicacy," Rapper kidded. Alex laughed.

"OK, I've got a joke," Alex said. A good dose of humor was needed after such a long ride. Paul and Rapper leaned in to hear it. Leaning was a privilege Paul had missed while wearing his suit of armor. Now the Superkids' suits were stacked over by the horses. They were in their tan T's, jeans and athletic shoes again.

"So this pastor asks a guy to paint the inside of his church. He gives him money for 10 gallons of paint and sends him out to buy it. The painter returns an hour later with *five* gallons of paint because he's pocketed the rest of the money."

Rapper chuckled. "Not too brilliant."

Alex continued, "So the painter gets about half the church finished when he realizes he's running out of paint. In a desperate attempt to finish the job, he thins the paint out with water, hoping to cover more of the walls. But it doesn't work."

"So did he tell the pastor?" Paul asked.

"Feeling awful," Alex said, "he comes clean. He goes to the pastor and says, 'I'm so sorry! Look at what I've done! I spent the extra money, thinned out the remaining paint and now the church looks awful! What will we do?!'

"And do you know what the pastor said?" Alex asked.

Paul and Rapper smiled, but shook their heads.

"He says, 'I'll tell you what you're going to do. You're going to *repaint and thin not!*'" Alex burst into a barrage of laughter with Rapper. Paul rubbed his forehead. "Ohhhh, Alex, that's ba-a-a-ad!" he exclaimed.

Paul observed the dark forest around them as their laughter waned. One of the horses nickered as it pawed the ground with a slap of its front hooves.

"What's he all stirred up about?" Rapper wondered, still smiling.

"Something wrong, fella?" Alex asked the horse.

"It's too quiet," Paul whispered. "I don't hear any crickets."

"So...maybe this is a cricket-less forest," Alex suggested, "though I thought I heard some earlier."

"Or maybe the dragon's coming to get us," Rapper said flippantly.

Paul shot his friend a glance. "Quiet, Rapper."

"C'mon, Paul," Rapper said. "What? Do you think he's going to break through the trees and swoop down on us? C'mon, ugly dragon!" Rapper yelled. "Give it your best shot!" Then he whispered, "I still think it's probably the size of a Chihuahua."

"Watch your words," Paul scolded. "Believe me, I know."

Suddenly, the sound of moving air brushed through the trees, eerily reminding Paul of the past night's visitor at the stable.

The horse stomped again and jerked its head up, agitated. It was anxious about something.

Paul felt a chill creep down his back.

He raised his head toward the treetops.

And he watched...as the sky was replaced with a dark, monstrous shape.

Paul's stomach twisted as a thick shadow blanketed the forest. The dark became darker, putting Paul, Rapper and Alex at an instant disadvantage. The fire threw dancing shadows in all directions.

"WHY ARE YOU HERE?!" a guttural voice pounded down at the adventurers. The words were like thunder, but clear enough to be understood. There was no mistaking them.

Paul looked at Alex, then Rapper, but could barely see either one. Darkness enshrouded them like long overcoats, from head to toe. Though his heart was beating faster than a tune from *D.J. Dizzy and the Space Cadets,* Paul remembered he was still the designated leader. He would answer the question.

"Uh," Paul's voice cracked, as he peered into the sky. "We're looking for a friend of ours. Her name is—"

"KELLIE..." the voice boomed, finishing Paul's thought. Hearing her name come from such an ominous voice made Paul shudder. "THE MAIDEN IS MINE. LEAVE MY KING-DOM NOW OR THIS NIGHT SHALL BE YOUR LAST."

Paul glanced over at Rapper and Alex again. *Holograms and mechanics,* he thought. Then he looked back up. "The maiden is not yours to claim!" Paul shouted. "Tell us where she is, let us have her and *then* we shall leave!"

The pause that hung in the air was long enough to make Paul wonder if he'd been heard. He realized the depth of his disadvantage: he was in unfamiliar territory, didn't know exactly where Commander Kellie was, and was trying to reason with a being much larger and stronger than himself.

"MAY IT BE SO," the voice suddenly boomed.

Paul blinked. *That was it? He's going to free her? That was all it took? Or...could it be that he was saying "May it be so...this night shall be your last"...?*

Fffffff!

With a burst of hot air, the campfire was instantaneously snuffed out in answer to Paul's question.

"I don't like this..." Alex whispered, his voice shaking.

"Hey!" Paul shouted, uncertainty quivering his voice. The comfort of the "holograms and mechanics" theory was quickly dissolving. "What are you doing?! Give us our fire back!"

"YOU WANT FIRE?!"

Something told Paul he shouldn't have asked for that.

BOOOOM! Like a bolt of lightning, a shaft of fire shot down from above and plummeted into the center of their extinguished campfire. The logs and twigs inside exploded out from the force. Paul, Rapper and Alex leapt backward, diving into the foliage.

Paul gazed up and watched the dark shape above dart up, then back down. Evil laughter boomed into the forest.

"HEH-HEH-HEH-HEH-HEH."

The horses shrieked and kicked, loosening their ties to the trees. Sparks of fire from the tossed logs leapt to the plant life, igniting everything in their vicinity.

BAM! Another surge of fire smacked the tree above Paul. He looked up just in time to see a large branch coming down at him. Instinctively, he rolled to the side as it smashed to the ground beside him.

Rapper was already up and running toward the horses. With a quick motion, he unwound their reins from the burning trees. Alex headed toward their armor, but retreated in a dive when a ball of fire cut off his path.

Paul still couldn't see the dragon. He was up there, but it was too dark to see. At times he thought he saw the blackness of the beast's nostrils when he breathed out fire, but it was too hard to tell. *Why did it have to be a dragon?*

The horses dashed for freedom the second their reins were loosed. Paul stood and ran, shouting for Rapper and Alex to join him.

"We need our swords!" Rapper cried back.

"Forget 'em!" Paul screamed. "Let's go! Let's go!"

Leaves dropped down like burning snow, melting to ash when they hit the ground.

BAM!

Rapper and Alex caught up with Paul and they took off in the direction they had come.

"The lake!" Alex shouted.

"Yes!" Paul echoed his excitement. "We can't be hit with fire under the water!"

"We can't stay underwater forever!" Rapper contradicted.

"It's better than being out here!" Paul shouted back. He looked up and saw the stars behind him disappear as the dragon flew overhead. It was difficult to see the beast because of the trees and the darkness...but he was still right behind them.

BLAM! Another stream of fire spilled down a tree in front of them, causing the boys to split up for a moment.

Then Paul heard it. Barely, but he heard it. Straight ahead. Lapping water. The lake where Alex had watered the horses.

Paul remembered it wasn't that big. It was actually more of a large pond. But it would do. It *had* to do.

POW! Another burst of fire hit Paul's heels.

"Hot! Hot! Hot!" he cried, but every step spread the fire behind him.

Just a few more steps and...

The three Superkids reached the edge of the lake and leapt up into the air. They sailed forward, defying gravity, but gravity won out and seconds later each one hit the lake.

SPLASH!

SPLASH!

SPLASH!

Paul's shoes extinguished as they went under. It was deep. Paul kicked and swam forward, staying under the surface. Rapper and Alex followed him closely.

Opening his eyes, Paul peered ahead, but couldn't see much. Then suddenly, it became much brighter. Paul glanced over his shoulder and noticed the balls of fire hitting the lake and extinguishing with a spurt. But each fireball gave them a few seconds glance at the underwater world.

Tiny fish darted left and right, their placid environment interrupted by an explosive surprise from the world above.

Paul, Rapper and Alex held themselves underwater with soft waves of their arms. Rapper pulled his hand toward his neck, held it flat and moved it side to side. Using a standard underwater hand signal they had learned at the Academy, Rapper was telling Paul and Alex he was out of air.

Paul thought for a long moment. He looked around as a few more fireballs hit the surface above.

Rapper pulled his hand toward his neck, held it flat and

moved it side-to-side again. He had to get up. He had to get air.

A silver fish caught Paul's eye. He watched it for a moment. Then he quickly whirled back around, his own lungs burning. He made a fist and held his thumb up, then raised his hand. Rapper and Alex acknowledged the signal and knew it was time to go up.

SPLOOSH! The Superkids burst through the water surface at once and all gasped for a big breath of fresh air. Paul looked to the sky and saw the dragon above, circling around.

"I think I saw a cave," he spat out between breaths. "I saw a fish go inside, but I don't know if it leads anywhere."

"It's better than staying here!" Alex pointed out. Rapper nodded.

"Get a big breath this time," Paul ordered.

The dragon discovered his enemies had returned and reared back. Paul could almost make out the dragon's long, muscular shape against the black sky...almost, but not quite. The firelight burning through the forest ahead of them revealed only the silhouette of the approaching beast.

At once a searing breath came from above, throwing a column of fire at the Superkids. The boys dropped down as the fire smacked the water and dissipated. Paul felt the heat on his back.

Paul gathered his bearings and looked at Rapper and Alex. He held his hand flat with his thumb on top and waved up and down toward the area where he had seen the cave. Rapper and Alex understood. He was pointing where to go. Quickly, the boys darted forward underwater. As they moved from the area where the dragon was targeting his fire, it became darker, but periodically they would get a burst of light.

Paul realized they had reached the edge of the lake when he

hit the soft mud with his head. He pulled back and held his hand in front of him steadily, signaling Rapper and Alex to stop. He spread out his fingers and moved his hand side-to-side, signaling that something was wrong. The cave wasn't there.

Alex pointed to the right with his finger then held his hand flat with his thumb on top. He moved his hand up and down. He had found it. Paul and Rapper followed Alex.

The water became colder and the boys were quickly surrounded by complete darkness. Paul felt unnerved. He was trying to calculate how far they could go before they wouldn't have enough air to get back to the surface behind them. Paul's chest was already beginning to hurt.

They kept going.

Paul realized they had passed the safety point. There was no way to turn back now. They'd never make it. Thoughts rushed through Paul's mind as he wondered if he should have led his friends to the lake. Maybe it wasn't such a good idea. Paul brushed the top of the cave and realized it was getting much narrower.

BAM! Paul hit Rapper and Rapper hit Alex. Alex had stopped for some reason. Then Paul saw it. It was a stone wall.

At first Paul felt like panicking, but amazement took over as he realized he could *see* the stone wall. Paul looked up. Dim, flickering light from the burning forest was coming from above. Paul started to point up, but Rapper and Alex were already heading in that direction.

Paul's lungs felt like they were ready to burst.

SPLOOSH! The Superkids broke the surface and gasped for air. Gasping echoed off the stone wall encircling them.

For five minutes no one said a word, but just gasped and wheezed and coughed for air.

"I think...we're...in a...well," Alex noted between breaths.

Paul knew Alex was right when he looked up and saw a wooden bucket dangling far above his head.

A few more minutes passed as they slowly treaded water and regained their breath.

Rapper let out a short laugh. "That was no Chihuahua," he said. "How did he find us anyway?"

Paul was taken a bit aback. "You can thank your corrupt mouth, for sure."

"What?!" Rapper questioned. "This is *my* fault?!"

"You sat there and *said* the dragon was going to find us—what you said was contrary to what you *should* have been saying. That's *corrupt*—believe me, I know."

Rapper looked like he was going to say something in return, but thought better of it.

"Guys, this is actually a positive thing!" Alex said with a toothy smile.

Paul and Rapper both turned to Alex.

"Positive?" Paul asked.

Alex nodded. "We suddenly have an advantage."

"What?!" Rapper shouted. "We're at the bottom of a well, in soaking clothes, without our armor, without our horses and without our map!"

"But," Alex noted, raising his finger out of the chilly water to make a point, "the dragon thinks we're dead."

Paul and Rapper looked back at each other and smiled. They hadn't thought about that.

Climbing up the long rope was extremely difficult after their swim, and Paul was exhausted when he made it to the top. Using the help of the well's crank, Paul raised Alex up to the top and Alex raised Rapper. When they were all finally on solid ground again, they let out a unified huff and slumped down by the side of the well.

In the distance they watched the forest burn, casting black smoke into the sky. The warm, night air began to dry the clothes on the Superkid's worn and tired bodies. One by one they drifted off into a deep sleep. They knew they couldn't take another step even if they wanted to.

The dragon had won the battle. But Alex was right. The Superkids suddenly had the advantage. The war wasn't over yet.

As the days pass, I have been wondering who is behind this mean-spirited kidnapping. And why me? Though I still have no answer for my first question, the latter has come to light.

From these small holes in the wall, the smell of burning wood crept in last night. At first I thought it possible that a camp-site may be nearby, but then I realized the stench was too strong for that. Something big has burned, I am sure.

This may somehow be related to a visit I received. Late last night I was awakened by a man wearing a long, brown robe. He was wearing the robe as a disguise, I'm sure—a hood covered his head. He even kept his hands in his pockets for the longest time so I wouldn't see his skin. But when I sat up, he pulled one hand out...a hand holding a laser gun. It was a standard RM-327. No clues there.

He came in to tell me "exciting news." According to him, my "rescue team has been eliminated." This, of course, made him quite pleased. At first, I was hit with shock, then sadness, then anger. But I will stand confident. I know this is why the Lord had me pray for Paul, Rapper and Alex. They must be the res-cue team the man spoke about. But I know by faith, regardless of his words, that my Superkids are safe. God's Word is more powerful than this coward who has jailed me.

But something else the robed man said made me curious. He said I am his "guinea pig" and he was disappointed I have made no effort to escape. Of course, this is not true, but I did not tell him that.

So I wonder, why does he want me to try to escape? I imagine the answer to this question will be revealed soon—very soon.

Kellie

✪ ✪ ✪

The soft sound of flute music drifted through the air like a cloud. Paul's eyes blinked open slowly as the tune soothed him. His mind gradually remembered the events that had led him to the spot where he sat. He lay slumped against the old, stone well, sitting up, with Rapper asleep on one side and Alex on the other. As Paul remembered more, his senses began to pick up the aches and pains in his body. His back was stiff, he had a crick in his neck and his legs and upper arms felt like jelly.

As he lifted his head and looked at the forest not so far away, sadness engulfed him. The trees were black, their leaves gone, and the ground was ash. Some burning embers lay here and there, threatening to start the fire all over again...if there were anything left to ignite.

Paul's eyes opened wide as he remembered the beast that had caused the trouble.

As if Paul's thought triggered the action, suddenly the dragon emerged from the forest beyond. His dark frame was a silhouette as it had been the night before—in spite of the rising sun. Huge wings that flapped like kites in the wind steadied the beast's course. He was headed straight toward Paul.

Paul glanced at his companions, still sound asleep. He tried to shout something, but his mouth was suddenly dry. His body was frozen against the well. The flute music became louder, ringing in his ears. The dragon drew closer and closer. Paul couldn't see its eyes...it was just a big, black blob coming at him.

A burst of flames exploded from the dragon's mouth and ignited the air into an atmosphere of fire. Paul slapped his hands up and down his body. He had to find a defense...but his sword was gone, his armor was gone—he was weaponless!

Then Paul saw his small Bible lying on the ground beside him. He picked it up and held it in front of him like a miniature shield. As the fire burst around him, the Bible deflected it, sparks dancing off the cover.

The scream Paul had been trying to release finally made it through his vocal cords.

"...aaaaaaaaaaAAAAAAAAHHHHHHHHHH!!!!"

Paul's eyes popped open as his own voice awakened him. He found himself sitting at the well, with his hands outstretched before him. Rapper and Alex were wide-eyed on either side of him.

Paul blinked.

The forest was the same as it had been a moment ago, burnt and black. But there was no dragon.

Paul put his arms down.

"I, uh...." Paul stammered, then said, "Just a dream."

Rapper shook his head. Alex patted Paul on the arm. "You have been promoted from leader to alarm clock," he joked.

Paul smiled.

The soft flute music still wafted through the air, piquing the Superkids' curiosity.

"What's that?" Alex inquired.

Rapper stood up. "Rads, we're rough. Are your clothes as stiff as mine?"

Paul nodded as he stood. "That's the least of our concerns," he noted. "We lost our horses and our armor—"

"—and we need to find our map," Alex added.

As if that weren't enough, Paul knew his companions had to be as hungry and thirsty as he was...but their food and drink were at their previous night's campsite.

With little effort, Paul convinced Rapper and Alex that they all had to try to find their camp.

The walk back was disheartening, to say the least. Not only was their sense of direction muddled by the recent events, but the forest was in ruins. The Superkids trudged through thick piles of ash, turning their athletic shoes black. Nearly two hours passed before they discovered the large pool they had dived into. Paul let out a long sigh. Their camp couldn't be far.

To Paul, it was strange to walk through the forest only a day later and find it was a completely different place. As they had traveled the day before, birds chirped, crickets sang and occasionally they saw other animals: a prancing deer, a scampering raccoon, a curious squirrel. But not today. Today the forest was silent...except for the soft music floating through the air. Every once in a while, they could still hear the flute.

"There!" Rapper shouted, pointing to the east. Paul saw it, too. On the ground were the large, chunky stones Paul had gathered to fence in their fire. They were no longer in the perfect circle he had made; the dragon's flaming breath had destroyed that. But they were the stones he had used. They had found their camp.

After digging through some piles of ash and soot, they

found the remains of their backpacks. The good news was that the rations were there with two of their water canteens. After another 10 minutes, Alex found the missing canteen, but it brought no blessing.

He lifted the last canteen in the air and held it upside down. A lone drop of water slid out and plopped into a pile of ash below. There was a hole popped in the edge of the canteen—and it had emptied. "Guess I'll wait," Alex muttered.

"I don't understand how a hologram could do this." Paul said.

Alex shook his head. "I told you guys: It's holograms *and* mechanics. Some of them—like the squirrel we saw when we came in—are just textured holograms. But other parts are more than that. There are mechanics underneath...hazardous mechanics *shrouded* in holograms."

"You know that makes no sense, don't you?" Rapper asked.

"It makes perfect sense," Alex responded pointedly. "We're seeing it with our own eyes. It's not only believable, but it's also dangerous. Someone has done a superb job creating this."

Paul added, "Too superb."

The Superkids sat down together and ate their breakfast, thanking God for helping them find it. Then each Superkid took a few gulps of water. Paul made a point of mentioning to use the water sparingly...the two canteens wouldn't last forever. Maybe another two days. Maybe three.

"We have to find Commander Kellie," Paul whispered, closing a canteen.

The next logical step, the Superkids agreed, was to find out where the flute music was coming from. Since their horses, armor, swords and map were missing from the camp, perhaps whoever was playing the music could lead them to their possessions. Paul was hoping so. He sure didn't want to try and locate the dragon and then fight him barehanded.

As they walked, the music became louder. The song of the flute had been carried by the wind, but Paul could hear other instruments now. A light drum, perhaps another flute and some kind of stringed instrument, Paul guessed. The song was slow and sad.

Rapper was the first to spot the rooftops ahead and Alex remembered the map had shown a village near their camp. This was Trenton! Perhaps someone could finally help them. Perhaps the inhabitants could lead them to the answers they needed.

The burnt blackness of the forest gave way to rich, green grass and a quaint, little town. The buildings were made of logs with hay and wood rooftops. A road that crept its way through the town was imprinted with horse's hooves and lines from cart wheels. Up ahead, Paul could see a couple of people glancing over and then staring at the oddly-dressed Superkid newcomers, probably not sure what to think.

The Superkids' first steps onto the green grass were more of a splash. The ground was soaked with water—the villagers' attempt at protecting their village from the previous night's blaze. The flute hit a sour note and a giggle emerged as Paul pulled his wet foot out of a puddle. He glanced over and saw the ensemble whose music had been tickling his ears. Three young women and two young men were sitting on midsize rocks, holding instruments.

The girl who had giggled, quickly composed herself and nodded to her troupe. Her face turned thoughtful as she blew into the mouthpiece of her instrument. Paul, Rapper and Alex froze in place as they listened to the beautiful, yet simply orchestrated music. It was clearer...and more sweet...now that they were closer.

Paul watched the young girl play her flute. Each breath flowed notes out of the instrument like liquid. The flute girl— who was near Paul's age—had black hair and brown eyes, which Paul hadn't noticed when he first saw her. Now her eyes were looking down. Next to her stood a younger girl, also playing a flute. Her instrument was smaller and thinner than the other, but just as melodic. As Paul had guessed, there were a couple of drums, played by a young man with curly, black hair. He was probably about 16, as was the third young man with straight, blond hair. This one played a lute, Paul surmised. He had never actually seen one, but he thought that's what the pear-shaped, guitar-like instrument was.

A fifth member stood still, contemplating. She, like the others, wore a brown overcoat. Quite a drab quintet. Then the fifth girl began to sing. And the music became even more beautiful. The Superkids listened closely to the sad song...

As a flame burneth wax down a candlewick
So doth our great wood ignite
The stars fade to blackness, thick
As the sun gloweth through the night

Destiny foresaw it best for us
To live or die as it wills
As Scratch submitteth his way of trust
One day shall our thirst be filled

"Dost thou fear Scratch?" Paul shouted aloud to the musical group. Rapper and Alex turned to their friend, surprised. The music came to an abrupt halt.

"What're you doing?" Rapper questioned Paul, staring ahead and smiling as if nothing was wrong.

"Getting us some allies," Paul answered out of the side of his mouth. He had an idea...one he was hoping would work.

"I ask thee a question!" Paul shouted at the group. "Deserve I not an answer?"

"Indeed," the young, blond-haired lute player answered. "Nevertheless thy question be no question should the answer be plain."

Paul nodded. Yes, the answer to his question *was* obvious. The people feared the dragon. Of course they did. The beast had just torched their entire forest with a sneeze.

"Allow me another," Paul submitted. "I dare ask, '*How much* dost thou fear Scratch?'"

Paul glanced at the girl who played the flute. She would not look up at him.

"Thou dost inquire again that to which the answer is plain," the lutenist replied.

"Do I?" Paul challenged.

"We fear Scratch with our very lives!" the lutenist shouted. "He rules as he wishes! Our lives exist for his demand! Should we live or die, 'tis up to Old Scratch."

"Nonsense," Paul said. The word shocked each of the band members. Even the flute girl's brown eyes popped up.

"Canst thou speak so bold?" the lutenist asked. "Who art thou and from whence dost thou come?"

Paul pointed back toward the edge of the forest. "If thou

truly believest Scratch may do as he wills, why didst thou stop his fire from consuming thee the night of last? Thou didst stop the will of Scratch with mere action!"

The lutenist, the flutist and the others stared back at the water barrier they had created at the edge of the forest. Paul hoped his message was sinking in. Perhaps they would see they weren't so happy with Scratch after all.

"Thou sayest truly...and bold," the drummer admitted softly.

"What wouldst thou have us do?" the lutenist questioned with a whisper. "And *who art thou?*"

Paul smiled. "I think we can help one other."

❂ ❂ ❂

"Friends! Romans! Countrymen! Lend me your ears!"

Paul and Rapper looked at Alex with raised eyebrows. When he said he knew how to call the town together for a meeting, Paul hadn't expected him to start quoting Shakespeare.

One by one, the townspeople gathered as Paul had wanted. Upon meeting, the weary people listened as Paul shared new ideas with them...visions of destroying the dragon together.

"Thou hast lived under the thumb of this tyrant too long!" Paul said. "Together, we can destroy Scratch."

The people were scared and unsure, but Paul felt as though he were getting through to them.

"How knowest we thou hast not been sent by the dragon himself?" one of the locals challenged.

Paul pointed back at the forest. "The fire of yesternight," he responded. "It cameth not because Scratch hateth thee, but because Scratch hateth *us.*"

The crowd murmured. A man worked his way through the

crowd and pointed at Paul. It was Andrew—and Paul was never so pleased to see someone.

"I testify to the truth of this knight!" Andrew shouted. Again the crowd murmured, asking among themselves, "This boy, a knight?"

"These three lodged with me a past night's hence. They be gentlemen and honest men."

Paul nodded a thank-you toward Andrew and briefly wondered if the kind friend was curious about his horses' whereabouts. Suddenly the crowd parted and a burly man headed through the sea of townspeople. He had a thick face and warrior markings on his arms. In his hands were three swords.

"Then of a truth, these be thine!" he shouted.

"Our swords!" Alex exclaimed.

The man dropped one sword to the ground and tossed another to Paul. The third he kept for himself.

"If thou be a knight, prove it," the big man challenged. Paul gulped.

"Actually," Paul said, wielding the sword and nodding to Rapper, "he's more the swordsman."

"Aaaaaggggggghhhhh!" the big man yelled as he ran forward.

Dashing to the right, Paul blocked the big man's blow. Paul came back at him with a twist of his wrist, but the man blocked Paul's effort.

Clang! Clang!

"From whence came these swords?" Paul asked as he shuffled around the man.

"When the fire began, I was in the great forest and heard the sound of thy horses." The man came forward with another swing. Paul lurched to the left this time. "As I drew near, I beheld thy swords and thy map."

Paul's biceps were feeling weak from the man's heavy blows. "What about our armor?" Paul wondered aloud.

The man shook his head. "Armor, hmmm? I saw it not."

Paul backed up at the next blow. He was getting tired fast. He began praying in the spirit under his breath.

The big man locked Paul's sword in a swing and pushed him to the ground. Paul hit the earth with a thump that knocked the wind out of his lungs.

"Thou callest thyself a knight?!" the big man mocked.

Suddenly the man's eyes grew big and he froze. Paul gasped as a sharp metal blade swiftly slid beneath the man's chin, giving him a close shave. Rapper leaned forward from behind the man, holding his sword steadily in place.

"Thou forgetteth," Rapper whispered into his ear, "we fight together, and 'tis our unity that proveth thy defeat."

The big man gulped as a smile popped up on Paul's face.

"You gotta love unity," Paul said, letting his "medieval talk" slide for the moment. "Now let's stop fooling around. We've got work to do."

Calling the Dragon

This place is more of a prison than I first imagined. It is built strong. From the inside it seems impenetrable. But things do change based upon one's vantage point. I pray that when Paul, Rapper and Alex find me, getting in will be easier for them than getting out has been for me. Meanwhile, it appears that whoever put this together has just what they wanted—a place impossible to escape.

I'm tempted to lose hope. But I refuse to give in to the temptation of the enemy. Time is wearing on and I am alone, but I won't stop speaking God's Word in faith. Proverbs 21:23 says, "He who guards his mouth and his tongue keeps himself from calamity." Therefore, I will guard my mouth and speak the Word. After all, it's about vantage point again. From in here, it looks hopeless. But how does God see it? No question there. He is the God of hope (Romans 15:13). And He will fill me with all joy and peace as I trust in Him, so that I may overflow with hope by the power of the Spirit.

Holy Spirit, make my hope overflow today...and each day that is to come.

Kellie

✪ ✪ ✪

"We just don't feel it's honest," Rapper stated, plain and simple.

Paul didn't like hearing those words. What wasn't honest? Paul had worked hard to mobilize the townspeople and help them realize they could fight the dragon. It had taken nearly two days to get everyone unified and working as a team. Now, just when he thought everything was ready to go, Rapper and Alex were having second thoughts.

So Paul asked, "What about this isn't honest?"

"What about it *is?*" Rapper suggested.

Paul looked around. The townspeople were busy carrying wood, pounding nails and setting traps for the dragon. Each night Old Scratch patrolled the village—flying over to make sure everything was just as he wanted. Well, this night Scratch was going to have a surprise waiting when he arrived.

"Well, I think it's great," Paul said, truthfully. "This way we can take out the dragon, rescue Commander Kellie and get out of here fast."

"That's our point," Rapper said. "You're not being totally honest with these people. You haven't even mentioned Commander Kellie. They think you just hate the dragon."

"I do hate the dragon."

"But we're not here to hate the dragon—we're here to rescue our commander."

"How is one different from the other?"

"Rad!" Rapper shouted, throwing his arms up in the air. "Hello?! We're almost out of food! We're almost out of water! And instead of using our resources to accomplish our mission, we're wasting them fighting the dragon!"

Paul folded his arms across his chest. He lowered his voice

to keep from attracting attention. "Look. We have our swords and map back," he said, "but our armor and our horses are gone. This may be our only opportunity. What? You want to walk up to the castle barechested and face that beast one-on-one?"

"I'd rather!" Rapper argued. "We at least need to be honest with these people. Let them know about Commander Kellie. Maybe they know another way to rescue her. Didn't Andrew mention another route to the castle?"

"Yeah, a treacherous one. Besides, if it was important to mention Kellie, Andrew would have said something to the people. And you're forgetting the most important point: *These are not real people. This is a computer simulation. Holograms and mechanics, remember?*"

Rapper nodded. "So it's all right to tell a lie so long as no one's really hurt?"

Paul shook his head. "It's not the same."

Rapper didn't respond.

Paul looked over at Alex. "You agree with Rapper?" he asked.

Alex shrugged. "I think he's right," he admitted.

Paul threw his foot forward and kicked a pile of pebbles, spreading them across the ground. Then he pointed his forefinger at his friends as he proclaimed, "I'm going to get this dragon." Rapper and Alex stood quietly. Then Paul dropped his finger and added, "No matter what it costs."

The Holy Spirit has brought me to my knees again. The Lord has shown me I must pray...and I must pray *now.*

Kellie

✪ ✪ ✪

Nightfall quickly approached. The traps were completely set. The people were finally ready. Paul glanced over at Rapper and Alex. He knew neither of his friends entirely agreed with his plan, but he also knew that since he was in charge, they would respect his decision. He knew he could count on them. Now there was nothing to do but wait.

Paul, Rapper and Alex were crouched down behind a small, stone wall. Behind them was a hay-and-wood hut like so many that lined the village road. Aside from a light or two, though, the area was dark and quiet. Paul knew the people he inspired were waiting in their assigned places. Just waiting. Waiting for that surprise moment they had imagined thousands of times by now.

Paul had been waiting and imagining, too. For years he had waited for this moment...the moment he could pounce on the dragon and give *him* a nightmare.

The village was quiet. The air was stale. The stars began to emerge above in a purplish, cloudless sky. Slowly, a light haze rolled in.

Then, as a sudden chill whipped through, Paul's mouth went dry. Far away, up in the sky, a small silhouette danced between the stars like a bat. From the corner of his eye, Paul saw Rapper and Alex place their hands on the hilts of their swords.

Paul heard someone whisper, "Scratch!" Others whispered nervously.

The closer the dragon drew, the larger he became. For a moment, Paul felt himself wanting to run, to change everything he had done. Maybe, he thought, bringing the dragon to the small village wasn't such a good idea. After all, had he really studied the beast's weaknesses? Had he ever even asked the

Lord how to handle such an animal? As the dragon drew even closer, Paul realized there was no time left for regrets. He pushed the troubling thoughts out of his mind and focused his attention on the task at hand. Paul grabbed the hilt of his sword, too.

The dragon drew closer.

And closer still.

Soon, it was almost on top of them.

It was the time Paul had waited for.

"Now!!!" Paul cried as his sword slid out of its leather scabbard and cut into the air.

The dragon stopped in midflight, surprised. In the darkness of night, he was still not much more than an ominous shape in the sky, but Paul could see the surprise in his movements. His tail swung underneath him as he pulled back in curiosity.

Pop! Pop! Pop! Pop! Pop!

Door-sized openings in the roofs of the huts dropped open. Light beamed out of the rooftops like square searchlights.

When the light hit the dragon's eyes, Paul gasped. The dragon's eyes were long and narrow like a cat's, but red in color. They blinked in anger as he surveyed the town. Thick, dark, brownish-green scales covered the lizard's body. An angry "V" of scaly eyebrows hung over his eyelids, making his stare ominous and evil. He had a long snout, and on the top of his head, two sharp, crooked horns extended backward. The dragon's body was still hard to make out to Paul, but it was enormous. Giant, bat-like wings rippled in the wind. And that thick, scaly tail swung back and forth between the dragon's four, thick legs and bony toes. The moment seemed to take an eternity to pass.

But then it happened as planned.

Thunk! Thunk! Thunk! Thunk! Like round rockets, large

boulders were catapulted out of the houses, through the roofs and straight at the dragon. Scratch hadn't anticipated the hidden attack and he roared as he swept to the side, attempting to dodge the onslaught. But it was no use. The dragon took one pelt after another.

Bam! Scratch flew right to avoid a boulder and slid directly into the path of another oncoming missile. Just as he was knocked backward, another boulder struck his left wing, snapping it back. Another boulder socked the dragon in the belly. Another pummeled his back.

Bam! Bam! Bam!

"NOOOOOOOOOO!" the dragon cried.

Easier than anyone imagined, the dragon was hit again, this time on the skull, and knocked to the earth. As he hit, the ground shook like a sudden, small earthquake. Scratch wailed, defeated, as a black wing furled up in reflex and then relaxed down over the dragon's head. The beast's moan drifted off and after a few moments, he no longer moved.

The village fell silent.

Paul couldn't take his eyes off the dragon. Like a gigantic elephant, he lay there on his side. They actually did it. They actually defeated the dragon.

They actually defeated the dragon!

Paul slowly raised to his feet along with Rapper and Alex. He was speechless. He never even had to use his sword.

One by one, the doors to the huts creaked open and the inhabitants peeked out, wide-eyed. The townspeople emerged, surprised and shocked, and stepped up to the huge beast lying at their feet. Some were teary-eyed with joy, others were just bewildered.

Then the whispering came.

"Be he dead?"

"The dragon movest not!"

"I knew we would slay him!"

"Yes!!!"

The townspeople cautiously gathered around the carcass of the dragon and observed him close-up for the first time without fear. Paul recognized the big man he had sword-fought pushing his way to the front of the crowd. The man boldly took a step toward the beast and touched the reptilian skin.

"'Tis cold," he announced, pulling his hand away quickly, "very cold."

Then a chilling, low-pitched laughter reverberated through the air.

"HEH-HEH-HEH-HEH-HEH."

Paul felt his stomach flip. *Oh no.*

"YOU THINK I'M COLD?" The black wing covering the dragon's head furled back. Paul heard the people gasp as Scratch winked his red eye. "LET'S SEE HOW COLD I CAN BE..."

Scratch, still on his side, flipped his front right foot forward and slapped the big man with his bony-fingered paw.

Fzzzzzappp! Instantly, the man vanished. Paul's mouth dropped in surprise. The townspeople screamed and ran as fast as they could for shelter.

The deep, roaring laughter continued as Scratch pushed himself up into a four-footed, standing position. His wings flapped in the air, blowing a chilled wind through the village.

Scratch lifted into the air and dropped back down, 10 feet closer, and slapped his paw out at the nearest victim.

Fzzzzzappp! This time a woman vanished.

"How's he doing that?!" Paul shouted at Rapper and Alex. Rapper shook his head.

"He has some sort of control over the holograms!" Alex figured. "By touching them, he has the power to end their program!"

Fzzzzzappp! Fzzzzzappp!

"We've got to do something," Paul cried, "before he tries to end *our* program!"

The townspeople fled to their huts with everything they had. Some closed and locked their doors, hoping for the best. Others emerged with another weapon they had prepared for the attack: flaming arrows.

Fzzzzzappp! Fzzzzzappp! Two more people were erased.

As Paul, Rapper and Alex ran for a better shelter, fiery arrows whizzed over their heads like birds.

Pow! Pow! Pow! Pow! The arrows hit the dragon in the chest, and he roared, furious. At once, Scratch reared up like a horse and let out a column of fire from his mouth. The fire plunged into the nearest hut and caught quickly on the dry hay. Immediately, the inhabitants ran out.

Fzzzzzappp! Fzzzzzappp!

"Nooooooo!!!" Paul cried. The village burned around him as Paul ran out into the road. He unsheathed his sword and held it up toward the dragon. Rapper and Alex ran out after Paul, trying to pull him out of Scratch's path, but Paul wouldn't move.

Fzzzzzappp! Fzzzzzappp!

The dragon drew close and gurgled out another throaty cackle as he shot his paw forward at Paul.

Clang! Paul's sword rang as it slammed against the dragon's bony fingers. Paul stumbled at the blow. Scratch roared when he realized Paul didn't disappear at his touch like the rest.

"I'm not a part of your program that you can eliminate!" Paul yelled above the cries and shouts.

"YOU!" Scratch roared, recognizing Paul from the night before. "YOU STARTED THIS!" Scratch reared back again. Paul's eyes widened. He was about to be engulfed in fire! He took off to the side just as the gathering of flames came down and exploded against the earth. Paul felt the heat hit behind him as he ran—he just escaped it.

The dragon bounded forward after Paul, slapping victims out of the way.

Fzzzzzappp! Fzzzzzappp!

Paul desperately looked for another water oasis to dive into, but couldn't find any.

"Umph!"

Paul reeled as he slammed into a running townsperson. Dazed, he pressed his hand against his head. The townsperson ran the opposite way. Paul knew he had to think fast! Behind him, Scratch laughed again and lifted his paw into the air. Paul gasped as five talons popped out of his fingers, like a cat. At once, Scratch dove as Paul whirled around to run. A claw barely caught Paul on the heel, throwing him to the ground. Paul grabbed his foot and cried out in pain.

Rapper and Alex tried to run forward to help their friend, but when Scratch saw them, he threw a wall of fire down between them and Paul.

Old Scratch smiled wickedly and drew his scaly eyebrows down, masking his eyes.

"I TOLD YOU KELLIE IS MINE!"

Suddenly, like a brush of cool water, Paul felt his body

receive instant refreshment. The pain in his heel vanished. Like an answer to someone's prayer, Paul felt strength burst through his being.

"No!" Paul shot back, wide-eyed and boldfaced. "The Scripture says in Revelation 12:11 that we overcome by the blood of the Lamb and the word of our testimony! And Psalm 118:17 says, 'I will not die but live! And I will proclaim what the Lord has done!!!'"

At Paul's words, Scratch roared, enraged, and plowed the air overhead with another pillar of fire. Without a moment's hesitation, Rapper and Alex took advantage of the distraction and ran in to get Paul. The Superkid was already up on his feet and running. When Scratch looked back down again, all three Superkids had disappeared.

As Paul, Rapper and Alex ran through dark brush, they heard the dragon roar again and angrily cast crackling fire high into the air.

8
Aftermath

I was up half the night in prayer. I prayed for several hours (I wasn't sure what to pray for, but the Holy Spirit prayed through me—Romans 8:26). Then something terrible happened—and I am overjoyed.

Sometime after midnight, still long before the sun arose, a terrible shrieking filled the air. It was like the roaring of a lion, but fiercer. Then at times, it sounded like a man...but a mere man could not make that kind of noise. My joy is full because I recognized the sound of the groaning. It was the sound of a pride bruised, a weakness exposed.

I don't know what happened last night, but I am sure of this: If that weakness can be identified by my rescuers, freedom is nigh

Kellie

✪ ✪ ✪

Like so many times already on this rescue mission, Paul found himself absolutely speechless. Standing in the center of the village with Rapper and Alex, Paul let his shoulders sag.

Like paper houses exposed to a match, nearly every

building was burned to the ground. Black char splattered the roads from the columns of fire tossed from Scratch's throat. Crackling embers outlined the huts' boundaries—making Paul's stomach upset.

Like the forest earlier that week, this town was just another victim of the dragon's whim. Perhaps Andrew and the musicians had been right, Paul thought. Perhaps Scratch really did do what he wanted in this world.

But it wasn't right.

It wasn't fair.

It wasn't real, either....

But it *felt* real.

The village was nearly silent today. No one had anything to say. Here and there a villager carried a blackened log from one location to another. This sort of cleanup was more therapy than it was useful. Paul let out a vulnerable sigh.

The patch of ground before him had a deep series of grooves plowed in it. They looked like small trenches. They were all over the village. This was Scratch's trademark. He scratched the ground...just as he scratched away lives. Paul thought of John 10:10, "The thief comes only to steal and kill and destroy." *Boy,* he thought, *isn't that the truth...*

Alex nudged Paul as they started down the road, feeling defeated. "Hey," he said, "it's only a simulation. It's not real. That's what we have to remember."

Paul stopped and turned to his friends. "Not real. Yeah, right. This is so 'not real' that we've been arguing about not having enough food to make it out of here in time. This is so 'not real' that if an angel's hand hadn't come between my ankle and that dragon's claw, I might not *have* an ankle right now." Paul shook his head. "I know. Holograms and mechanics. But these are the most real—the most lethal—holograms and mechanics I've ever seen." Paul bit his lip. What else could he say?

"It's just not right," he added. "A simulation like this shouldn't exist. Who has the right to make something so life-threatening and then force someone to live here? Commander Kellie isn't here because she was looking forward to a vacation. This is no amusement park. It's no movie. Commander Kellie is trapped in here. *We're trapped in here!*"

Neither Rapper nor Alex said a word. They didn't need to. Paul turned back around and then jumped back in surprise.

Before him stood the flute girl—the one with the black hair and the brown eyes. But her eyes weren't soft this time.

SLAP! Paul's head jerked back with the blow to his face. He reeled as the girl came at him with another hit—this time to his chest.

"You did this!" she cried, tears pouring from her eyes. "You ruined everything! You brought Scratch's anger on us! We were peaceful! We were peaceful!"

"Scratch was wrong!" Paul tried to console. Rapper and Alex just watched, stunned.

"*You* were wrong!" the girl shouted. "I lost my brother to Scratch! I lost my brother!" The girl let out a last scream of anger and then collapsed into Paul's arms. Paul tried to remind himself that she wasn't real, her words weren't real, but his heart still sank. As her tears stained his shirt, Paul felt his blood begin to boil. This wasn't right. It just wasn't right!

Paul squeezed his eyes tight and pushed the girl away. The feeling of the others near him closed in on Paul. He had to get away—now! Paul took off down the village road, straight toward the blackened forest. He just had to get away. It wasn't right! It wasn't his fault!

Reaching the forest, the Superkid unsheathed his sword and sliced the air before him. He ran at a burnt tree and hit it with the blunt side of the sword. His weapon rang in the air. Paul dropped his sword on the ground and hit the tree with his hands one, two, three times, and then fell into it and crumpled to the ground.

Paul looked up at the sky, still hazy with smoke from the night before. It spun above his head, as if he were in a gigantic washing machine. Paul buried his face in his hands and shook.

Was this really his fault? Was he the one who caused this? He was the one who talked the townspeople into his ridiculous plan. He was the one who smarted off to the dragon in the forest. He was the one who wasn't doing his job when Commander Kellie was caught. He was the one not watching his words. He had done it. The flute girl was right. This *was* his fault. If he, Commander Kellie, Rapper and Alex all died in this mixed-up world, it would be because of Paul. No one else was to blame. Not even Scratch. Paul had done this. Paul West.

"Paul"—that was his name. He thought it ironic that it meant "small." How appropriate. That's exactly how he felt at the moment: Small in the world—so small.

Yes, Rapper, Paul thought, *you were right. This* wasn't *about rescuing Commander Kellie. This was about destroying a dragon that haunted me when I was young.*

Paul knew he had lost focus. He had lost sense. He threw his head back on the dead tree and listened to the air. It was quiet. He looked at the branches above him and sighed.

You're small, but I'm big in you.

The words startled Paul. He looked around to see if someone was there. But no one was. The words had come up in his spirit—strong.

Paul smiled weakly for the first time in a while. It had never bothered Paul that his name meant "small." It helped remind him how big Jesus was. It reminded him that he couldn't make it alone. He *needed* Jesus. That never changed.

"How do I make it through this?" Paul whispered to heaven.

How have you made it through other hard situations? the Holy Spirit whispered to his heart.

Paul thought. The answer was easy. He glanced down at his sword.

"Your Word is my sword," Paul said, thinking of Ephesians 6:16-17, "and faith is my shield."

The image of the dragon rearing up when Paul quoted the Word the night before flashed through his mind. It was like the dragon couldn't stand it when Paul spoke the Word.

Another scripture popped into Paul's thoughts: Hebrews 11:3. Paul pulled out his pocket Bible and read. The verse said that the worlds were formed by the Word of God. Paul turned back to Hebrews 1:3 and read that all things are upheld by God's Word.

Paul closed the Bible as he thought about what the Holy Spirit was saying to him. He thought about this world—the holographic one. It had been formed without the Word. And it wasn't upheld by the Word. Paul nodded. If things can only truly exist *with* the Word, then the holographic world was destined to fall. And if Paul had anything to do with it, it would fall hard.

After pocketing his Bible, Paul picked up his sword and

carefully slid it into its scabbard. Yes, he, Rapper and Alex would overcome by the Word. *That was the key. That was the dragon's weakness—he didn't have the Word. The holographic world had been created without it...and it couldn't stand up to it.*

Paul stood up and confidently squeezed the leather hilt of his sword. He had to get back to the others.

Everything suddenly makes sense—infuriating sense. After not much sleep last night, I was awakened by the robed figure again. He slipped in, offering fruit on a tray. But this time I was ready for him. Before he knew what was happening, I leapt up and grabbed his hood, exposing the face inside. I wasn't surprised by the face I saw. I knew him.

Kellie

✪　✪　✪

"How on earth did I miss this?" Alex was saying, rubbing his temples with his palms.

Paul, upon returning to the village, mobilized his friends and the three of them were ready to start their final attempt at rescuing their commander. It was their final attempt because the boys were nearly out of food and water. If this didn't work, nothing would.

Alex was still shaking his head as Paul and Rapper leaned over his shoulders and looked down at the map he had spread out over the ground.

"What did you miss?" Rapper asked. Alex pointed down at the bar code on the map. The bar code had been on Alex's mind for quite some time. He couldn't figure out what it meant, or what it was for. Apparently he had figured it out.

"Look at it closely," Alex offered. Paul and Rapper did.

"So?" Rapper said. "It's just a funny-looking bar code."

Alex took the map and turned it around 180 degrees—completely upside down. Paul looked at the bar code again.

"That's no bar code," Rapper whispered. Paul knew he was right. It was an emblem—the lines barely thinned at the edge of each letter. But they *did* thin. And the letters spelled "NME."

✪ ✪ ✪

Lo and behold, the face behind the shroud was none other than that NME troublemaker himself, Major Dread.

I asked him why he brought me here and why he was holding me against my will. Of course, since NME is out to stop God's Word from being spread, I figured I already knew the answer. Actually, I was quite surprised.

It seems NME has developed this place as a new kind of "Jail" for criminals. It's a high-tech holographic environment, Dread explained proudly, where NME can create whatever kind of atmosphere they want. I am party to a simulation of medieval times. He said I was in the main castle, guarded by a dragon (this must be what I heard last night).

I was brought here unwillingly because NME wanted to test their ability to keep someone with a strong will confined. So far, it seems to be working well, though I'm unnerved by the whole situation. This place is almost <u>too</u> real. It's not merely solitary confinement—it's dangerous.

Dread even bragged again that he had created an "undefeatable force" that destroyed my rescue party. But I believe they're fine. NME's major downfall has always been pride. And one of its sins is lying.

Now more than ever, I'm looking forward to leaving this place. Then we'll look at finding a way to stop this sort of entrapment from ever happening again. Meanwhile, I will wait and pray.

Kellie

✪   ✪   ✪

Paul slapped the map. "How could we not have seen this?"

"Got me," Alex said. "But things are beginning to fall into place."

Paul and Rapper looked up at Alex.

"When the Lord led me to this map," Alex continued, "I heard a couple of guys talking. I couldn't see them, but I knew I'd heard their voices before. Now I know where I'd heard them. It was when Mashela captured me and NME held me in that holographic room," Alex explained. "I heard their voices there. It was Major Dread and someone he called 'Professor.'

This whole thing links back to NME. And I thought *those* holograms were good."

"That explains why they kidnapped Commander Kellie," Rapper posed. "NME is against everything Superkid Academy is for—namely, spreading the Word."

"And it's by God's Word that we're going to get through this," Paul said boldly. The Superkids nodded.

Alex smiled. "Well, needless to say, the map makes a whole lot more sense now." Alex pointed to a long, squiggly line. "This is the river we saw when we came in." He traced it upward. "About a mile from here, if that, we can catch it upstream and then follow it toward the west and double back to the castle."

"But isn't that the way Andrew said was treacherous?" Rapper pointed out.

Alex pointed at some jagged lines on the map. "It is, but we've already learned that if we go straight toward the front of the castle, we'll be in the area where Scratch makes his rounds...and we're sure to be spotted. It's quite a distance, but if we follow the river, it should be easy." He pulled his finger across the map. "We'll have to go through a canyon here, cross the river here and"—Alex tapped the dark castle—"then face whatever's at the castle."

"Scratch," Paul whispered. Then he looked up at the others. "Look, I know I've been a bit fervent about all this stuff with the dragon, but things change *now*. Our first priority is rescuing Commander Kellie. If the dragon interferes, yes, we'll have to do whatever it takes. But if at all possible, I'd like to rescue the commander without running into Godzilla again."

❂ ❂ ❂

With swords at their sides and courage in their hearts, the three adventurers began the final leg of their journey. As they walked, Paul kept them quoting scriptures to keep their hearts and mouths full of the Word.

"Joshua 1:9—We are strong and courageous! We will not be terrified! We will not be discouraged! For the Lord our God is with us wherever we go!"

"Second Timothy 4:17—The Lord stands at our side and gives us strength!"

"Psalm 19:14—May the words of our mouths and the meditations of our hearts be pleasing in Your sight, Lord!"

In a short time, the Superkids found the river marked on the map. It was the same river they had seen when they first arrived. Paul reached down and scooped up a handful of water. The coolness felt wonderful on his hands. He threw it into his mouth and felt the sensation of wetness splash his tongue, but when he closed his mouth, the holographic water vanished inside.

"That's the strangest feeling," Paul admitted. Rapper chuckled.

Following the river, the boys walked for four hours, under the shade of trees, keeping their pace steady. Paul found himself thankful for the constant physical conditioning he received at Superkid Academy. Being in shape was essential for missions like this, when anything less would put them at a disadvantage. Several miles later, after two breaks and some water, Alex pulled out their map. He looked down at it and then looked northeast. "Those are the cliffs we have to cross," he said, pointing. "Then we double back only a short way and we're there."

Ahead was a series of large hills and sharp cliffs. It looked oddly dry in the otherwise healthy environment. The rocks were dark red. Some had an orange tint. All were disheartening.

"We don't have much left to drink," Rapper warned. Paul nodded. He already knew that.

"We are strong and courageous," Paul said. "Let's go."

In single file, the Superkids began their trek up the hills. As they climbed, Paul noticed the many sharp scratches in the rocks. They were deep and reminded Paul of what he had seen in the village ruins. Paul realized that the dry hills were Scratch's playground—an area the dragon deliberately created to keep intruders from coming near the castle. The rocks were sharp, the ground was as stone. A perfect barrier.

The boys climbed the first hill with relatively few slips; the next two were more difficult. At one point, Paul looked at his rough hands and saw they were covered with the reddish residue from the rocks.

The sun beat down on the adventurers, making each step harder than the last. But they were determined. They just kept quoting the Word and receiving their strength from the Lord. And they kept remembering Commander Kellie. She wouldn't give up on them...and they weren't about to give up on her.

Paul froze when he came to the next obstacle in the dry hills. A long, narrow cliff jutted out in front of them. Paul knew there was no alternative—they would have to cross. He turned and looked at his friends. They nodded back. Paul took a step forward. The cliff's rocky ledge crumbled lightly under his weight. Small pebbles dropped straight down. It was about a 30-foot drop—farther than Paul was comfortable slipping.

Paul repositioned himself and grabbed hold of the cliff face, putting his back to the expanse below. He shuffled sideways.

Alex followed close behind, his back to the expanse, shuffling. Rapper came next. Pebbles broke away, cascading down.

"Only halfway to go!" Paul encouraged his friends.

Whump!

Rapper's foot slapped against the thin, rocky path and plowed straight through it. Rapper went down.

"Aaaaaaaahhhhhhhh!" With a thump, Rapper's hands grabbed the cliff ledge and he hung there for a second before shouting a weak, "Help!"

"Get him!" Paul shouted to Alex.

Alex tried to reach down, but couldn't bend with the rock face in front of him.

"I can't!" Alex cried. He looked over his shoulder and down at Rapper.

"I...can scoot the rest of the way with my hands," Rapper stated, not looking down.

"It's too far," Paul countered. "We still have a way to go. We have to get you back up on the ledge!"

"I mean the *other* way!" Rapper cried. "I can get back to the side we came from."

One hand after the other, Rapper slowly slid himself back. Paul's own heart was beating fast. He glanced over his shoulder and looked down. His head swam as he realized how far it was.

"You can do it!" Paul shouted to his friend.

Rapper finally made it, found a foothold and climbed up. He slid back onto the narrow ledge again, pausing to regain his strength and catch his breath. Paul, Rapper and Alex let out a long sigh of relief. As soon as Rapper was ready, the trio continued.

"Watch how hard you step," Paul warned. Then he turned to continue his shuffle across.

"Well, it certainly can't get worse than that!" Rapper said with a grin. Paul continued along the ledge until he reached the other side. Sliding his foot onto more solid ground, he helped his companions the rest of the way across. When all three had made it, they looked straight ahead at the dark castle, only a short distance away. They were almost there. From where they stood, it appeared mammoth.

Thick, black bricks made up the walls and the crooked turrets, with simple, small holes in the sides for windows. The grass surrounding it was plush green. Commander Kellie was in there—Paul could sense it in his spirit.

Then the Superkids looked down at what was between them and their goal.

Water. A wide expanse of the rushing river. And they had to cross it.

✪   ✪   ✪

After the three friends rested for a moment, Rapper admitted, "That's some moat." Paul and Alex nodded.

Down from the rocky terrain of the last cliff, the wide river ran as far as the Superkids could see. Paul was sure it was the same river they had followed earlier, but much more rapid at this spot. Water flowed past them quickly, rocketing downstream. The banks on either side were muddy and about 75 feet apart. Paul knew if they tried to swim it, they would be pulled downstream.

"That water sure is going fast," Alex pointed out.

Paul squinted toward the distant edge of the river. "Wait a second," he noted. "Look at that."

At the edge of the river bank was a beaver dam. With several long logs and intertwined twigs, a family of beavers had built a wide, thick dam that stretched nearly three quarters of the way across the river. The water rushed around it on the far side.

"Think we can walk across it?" Paul questioned.

Alex shrugged.

"Why not?" Rapper said.

The Superkids walked down the side of the cliff and approached the dam. The closer they drew, the louder the rushing river became.

"We have to watch ourselves," Paul cautioned. "If we fall in, it could pull us so fast we won't be able to get back out."

Alex looked at the map. "That'd put us back where we started."

"Not a good thing," Rapper added.

"Definitely not," Alex agreed.

Finally beside the dam, Paul bravely took the first, creaking step. "According to Luke 10:19, Jesus has given me the power to trample on serpents and scorpions and nothing shall harm me."

A moment later, he announced, "It's supporting me." He took another step. "Still good." Another three steps and Paul smiled widely. "Hey guys, looks like Old Scratch's obstacles aren't that treacherous after all."

Rapper stepped onto the dam next. Paul continued on his way. Next on was Alex.

One slippery step after another.

"This isn't so bad," Paul shouted back, careful not to lose his balance on the logs and debris.

Paul's next step landed softer, to his surprise. "The dam's soggy up here," he shouted back. Rapper and Alex froze in their steps.

"What?" Paul asked.

Alex pointed down at the log Paul stood on. "Th-that's no log!" Alex exclaimed.

Paul looked down just in time to see crooked, brownish teeth emerge from the water. He jumped back onto another log and let out a yelp when the alligator he had stepped on slithered out of its hiding place. Suddenly, trampling on serpents and scorpions took on a whole new meaning. The reptile flipped backward to face Paul and snapped down on air.

"Yikes!" Paul cried.

Pop! Pop! Pop! Three more gators at the front edge of the dam slid out and flipped around to face their prey. "Get off the dam! Get off the dam!" Paul cried. But no one moved.

"They're surrounding us!" yelled Rapper.

Paul whipped out his sword. He looked around him. "Knock out the logs!" he ordered. "We have to push the gators into the current!" Paul chopped at the log directly in front of him. As he sliced through a thick branch, the log twirled just as an alligator leapt on it. The alligator was swept under the water. The log broke free, catching the current, and sweeping the alligator downstream.

Rapper and Alex followed Paul's advice and went for the logs with their swords. *Chop! Pow!* Three more logs were loosed. Another alligator was swept back.

Number three came up on Alex from behind.

"Jump up!" Paul shouted. Alex leapt in the air instantly as Paul cracked down on the wood pile behind him. The swift river, now breaking through the center of the dam and running over, swept up the debris and the alligator that was on it. He didn't flow as far as the others, but far enough to be out of the way.

"Where's the fourth one?!" Paul demanded.

Rapper didn't lose a beat. "Behind you!"

Paul launched into the air just as a hungry snout came down near his foot. He lashed out with his sword. The logs in front of him cracked on impact, but the alligator lost no ground. Paul cracked down on them again. The alligator moved straight underneath him.

Avoiding snaps, Paul wedged his sword in the wood and rocked it back and forth with all his might. The log finally broke in a sudden torrent and Paul's entire footing was swept away. The alligator was tossed back and into the flow of water. Paul slipped down and let go of his sword. He grabbed the dam's edge as his body was pulled by the river's rage. Rapper and Alex hurried over and grabbed his wrists, helping him back to safety. They pulled hard, drawing their friend back up on the dam.

Without even a moment to take a breather, the three Superkids ran the rest of the distance across the dam. At the end, they had to leap as far as they could to the muddy riverbank on the other side. Each Superkid made it, to their delight, and collapsed on the grass.

"We made it!" Alex said between breaths.

"You're getting pretty good with that sword," Rapper complimented Paul.

Paul raised and looked downstream. The logs and the alligators were floating away with the rushing current...and his sword was nowhere to be seen. He dropped his head back onto the grass. They'd made it.

Alex suddenly sat up. "Do you hear that?"

Paul had his eyes closed. "What *now?*"

"It sounds like...Commander Kellie."

Paul's eyes popped open.

Paul, Rapper and Alex, despite their fatigue from the dry, treacherous hills and the turbulent river, raced to the side of the castle. Paul pressed his face against one of the open holes and looked down. At the bottom, he could see Commander Kellie looking up at him, smiling. Paul shoved his right hand through one of the openings. There was no way he could reach her, but somehow he felt closer. Down below, Commander Kellie lifted her right arm toward him.

"Commander Kellie!" he shouted. "We found you!"

"Thank You, Jesus!" Commander Kellie exclaimed, looking up. Rapper and Alex pressed their faces into the remaining two holes.

"Commander, I'm sorry for the foolish way I let my mouth go. I should have guarded my words—I apologize for all this!"

Commander Kellie smiled below. "Paul, I'm just glad to see you now. I knew you three wouldn't give up on finding me."

"Yo, where are you?" Rapper asked, politely trying to keep them moving.

"I'm not sure exactly," Commander Kellie responded. "But I think I'm at the top of a long flight of stairs."

"Well, we'll figure out where you are once we get inside," Paul said. "But don't be concerned—we'll find you. We didn't come this far to turn back now."

Commander Kellie suddenly spun around. "Someone's coming! I hear footsteps!"

The Superkids pulled back and ducked. Paul heard the door on the other side, down below, creak open.

✪　✪　✪

Commander Kellie moved toward the door, eager to draw attention away from the Superkids just outside the holes above.

"Major Dread!" she said loud enough for the Superkids to hear. "What an unexpected surprise."

Dread wasn't dressed in his medieval robe this time. With his cover exposed, he was wearing his usual, black, NME command uniform.

"I just came to say, goodbye, Commander Kellie."

"Goodbye?"

"Yes," Dread said, smiling devilishly. "Why don't you have a seat?"

"I think I'll stand."

"Our testing is complete," he boasted. "You were unable to escape and your rescuers have been...*destroyed.*" Dread punched the last word for impact.

Commander Kellie shook her head. "I don't believe it, Dread." She turned her head for a long pause and then turned back. "So now that you have what you want, why not just let me go?"

"Aw," Dread mocked, "if it were up to me, I'd let you go. But, you know how it is. The chain of command and all. General Fear says you stay. After all, with you out of the way, the rest of Superkid Academy will soon crumble."

Commander Kellie's eyes held steady. "Superkid Academy will never fall," she stated.

Dread smiled again. "So I'm leaving," he said, pointedly. "You can stay here as long as you can last. And keep in mind that even if you do make it through this door," he pointed to the door by which he entered, "the dragon I programmed is on the other side."

Commander Kellie's right eyebrow arched. "Dragon?"

"You can take your chances against him if you like."

Dread burst into a chilling laugh and exited the room. Commander Kellie heard him lock the door behind him. Immediately she turned around.

✪   ✪   ✪

"I *knew* it was NME!" Alex said.

"We'll get you out, Commander," Paul promised again.

"Was he telling the truth?" Commander Kellie asked. "Is there a dragon? Have you seen it?"

"Up close and personal," Rapper responded.

Commander Kellie let out a long breath. "Well, it's not stronger than Jesus in us," she said. Then, "I must be near its lair. Do you know where that is?"

Paul shared glances with Rapper and Alex. "Well," Paul said, "judging by the size of the dragon, it shouldn't be hard to find."

Saying quick goodbyes, the Superkids stood and departed, sneaking around to the front of the castle. Behind them, they heard their leader pray Psalm 91 for their safety.

✪   ✪   ✪

Paul, Rapper and Alex made it around to the front of the castle just in time to see Major Dread exiting through a tall, wooden door. In the distance, in the direction he was heading, they could see a horse waiting. No doubt he was going to "ride off into the sunset," never to return. Part of Paul wanted to follow him, to find out how he would escape the simulation, but he knew that would be counterproductive. As much as Paul didn't like admitting it, he knew it might take all three of them to free the commander from the castle.

Paul motioned for Rapper and Alex to wait behind. Quickly, he sneaked around to the front and slid through the wooden door Dread had just exited, catching it before it shut tight. He waited inside for about two minutes, in the dark, and then slowly pushed the wooden door back open. Major Dread was gone. Paul motioned for his friends to join him. Rapper and Alex came quickly.

"Let's not forget something," Alex whispered.

As their eyes adjusted to the dark room, Paul listened.

"On the map, this castle is the geographic center of the simulation," Alex said. "So, it stands to reason that the central computer system running this simulation is in the center of this castle."

"You think you can find it?" Paul pressed.

"I can do all things through Christ," Alex quoted Philippians 4:13. "I believe ending the simulation could be as easy as flipping the right switch."

"You mean you might be able to make all this disappear with a flick of your wrist?" Rapper asked.

"Every computer has an on/off switch," Alex explained simply. It made sense to Paul. Somewhere deep in the heart of the castle there had to be a plug they could pull, figuratively speaking. Now all they had to do was find it.

"OK," Paul said, "here's the plan. We're going to head to

the center of the castle. Alex, you look for that switch you're talking about. Rapper, you and I are going to find the commander. Agreed?"

The Superkids nodded.

The castle was unexpectedly void of activity. There were no sentries to sneak past, no servants from whom to hide. This struck Paul as odd, but even more odd was the fact that the castle, for the most part, had no rooms. As their eyes adjusted, Paul was the first to walk up a short series of steps. At the top, he realized that the steps simply led them into a long hallway. The inner wall of the hallway was perfectly curved. Paul followed the curve around. It made a huge, perfect circle. Paul imagined if he were flying above the castle, and there were no ceiling, the castle walls would look like a gigantic square, with a gigantic circle inside.

"So it's a circle," Rapper said, "How do we get inside it?"

"Let's keep walking," Paul said. Soon, the Superkids were back where they started. Paul was thankful that at least there were more of those small, cut-out windows in the outside walls so they could see.

"There must be something around here that triggers a door for us to walk through," Alex suggested.

"You've read too many mysteries," Rapper said flatly, stepping back and resting his foot on a rock. Suddenly, a grinding sound filled the room. Rapper jumped forward, off the rock. The rock continued to slide down and then a large section of the floor slid aside.

Before they understood what was happening, a trap door in the floor was revealed, with stairs leading down.

Paul's eyebrows popped up. "Apparently NME has read a

lot of mysteries, too." Rapper scratched his head.

One after another, the Superkids marched down the steps with Paul in the lead. The steps gradually descended, wrapping around the curved, inside wall. Each step echoed as they walked, but the three friends stayed quiet. Each half turn placed them in greater darkness until, after a descent of at least seven flights, they reached the bottom.

The air was thick and musty and smoky, like the air near the downdraft of a bonfire. It burned with the stench of sulfur. Paul coughed lightly, then turned and jumped. He almost let out a cry, but it was stifled by the thick air.

Standing before the Superkids were three tall knights, each in shiny armor. They could barely see the knights, but there was light in the room...coming from somewhere near. Paul's heart slowed down as he realized the knights bore a startling resemblance to...

"Those are our suits," Alex whispered.

It was true. Upon closer examination, Paul realized all three had the blue feathers proudly jutting out of the helmets, and the feet were set in cement.

"Now we know where our armor went," Rapper whispered.

"They're trophies," Paul said flatly.

The three suits of armor were the only trophies there, understandably. Paul, Rapper and Alex were most likely the first visitors to such a place...but if they didn't accomplish their mission, the room could one day be full of trophies. Paul shuddered at the thought of row after row of empty armor suits. He couldn't let that happen.

Paul caught himself. He knew he had to keep his focus. He wasn't there to battle the dragon that used to give him nightmares. He was there to rescue his commander...his friend. Still, he couldn't help but wonder—could that be done without confronting the dragon? A vision of the dragon rearing up on his hind legs and spitting fire at Paul flashed through his mind. *Well,* Paul thought, *avoiding another confrontation would be nice, anyway.*

Paul nodded. "Old Scratch can have these," he offered. "They can remind him of the three knights who just wouldn't die."

Paul, Rapper and Alex, staying close, followed the circular, inner wall around again. This time, about halfway around was a wooden door similar to the one they had entered on the outside of the castle.

Paul put his hand on the handle. "This is it," he whispered. "let's find out what's in the center."

"I hope, the central computer system," Alex said.

As the door creaked open, natural light hit the Superkids' eyes along with the sting of smoke. A sulfur smell, the strongest they had smelled yet, also hit them in the face.

"I don't like this," Rapper muttered.

A bit reluctant, Paul slipped through the door.

The room was gigantic. *This was the castle.* From the floor to the towering, open ceiling, the black brick formed a mammoth cylinder. Scattered on the floor were hay and rock and debris. And all over the chamber were scratches. On the wall, on the floor, on the door. Everywhere. Paul expected to see bones, too, like in the movies. But wiping holographic beings out of existence didn't leave bones. Directly across the way, Paul could see an open hall, down low, with several steel computers blinking and buzzing. On the far left was a set of stairs, crawling up the wall like a fire escape, and at the top, a door.

But truthfully, Paul barely noticed the details. Rapper and Alex overlooked them too. It wasn't hard to do. Their focus instead was on the monstrous, dark, brownish-green dragon sleeping in the center of the chamber.

With the light filtering down into the chamber, Paul could see Scratch clearly for the first time. Like a feline curled on its side, the dragon slept with his muscular legs buckled and his enormous head relaxed on his front claws.

Dark, brownish-green scales played over the beast's body, from the tip of his nose to the point of his snake-like tail. Paul noticed the angry "V" of scaly eyebrows was still there—even in his sleep—casting dark shadows over his eyelids. Crooked, gray horns extended back from his head, making his long snout look even longer. Paul hadn't noticed the small, single horn between the dragon's flaring nostrils before. Lengthy, thin, reptilian tendrils clinging to his chin were spread out on the floor. And his bony fingers were curled.

Down the dragon's spine, thin, but tall, fins were evident to the end of his tail. Like a vulture's wings at night, his black, webbed wings were closed, rippled at each side of his body. The closer his scales were to his belly, the lighter they became. Paul shivered. He could hear the beast snoring softly.

"He's huge," came Rapper's awed voice from behind. Paul nodded. The fierce creature was easily twice the size of an elephant...or more.

"Greater is He that is in us," Paul whispered back 1 John 4:4. The Superkids behind him remained silent. Paul wondered if there would be a way to retrieve their armor...but then he remembered it was now in cement. No, they would have to do this wearing only T-shirts, jeans and athletic shoes.

Paul waved his hand backward, motioning his companions to back out the door. Leaving the door cracked, Paul gave them instructions on the other side.

"OK, let's try to do this without waking him," Paul whispered as quietly as he could. "Alex, there's a computer area behind the dragon that—"

"I have to sneak around the dragon?!" Alex interrupted.

"We *all* have to sneak around the dragon," Paul countered. "All that's *in* that room is the dragon. We don't have a choice. But if you can shut down the whole system over there, the dragon and the castle and everything should disappear, right?"

"Well, the holograms will, but not the mechanics…but, yeah, it should shut everything down."

"Good enough. Rapper?"

Rapper nodded.

"You and I need to sneak to the far side and get to the top of the stairs. I imagine Commander Kellie is up there. She said she thought she was at the top of a staircase and it's the only one in the room. That's probably it. Since she had windows in her room, she had to be at least that far up."

Rapper took a deep breath. "Another flight of stairs," he whispered, rubbing his thighs. "Great."

Paul smiled, though he wasn't sure why. "If you need to communicate, use our underwater gestures."

Rapper and Alex gave him "OK" signs. Paul grabbed his friends' shoulders and closed his eyes.

"Father God," he prayed, "we come to You in agreement. We know we're not going in there alone—You're with us according to Matthew 18:20. We enter into the lion's den in Your courage and strength. Lead us and guide us, Holy Spirit. We're trusting in You for the answers we need. In Jesus' Name."

"Amen," Rapper and Alex agreed.

Alex led first. One foot in front of the other, Alex tiptoed around the dragon's head, then its body. Relatively easily, to Paul's delight, Alex made it to his destination. Paul could see him scanning the computer system, looking for something that resembled a shut-off switch.

Paul motioned to Rapper, who moved forward and led the way to the stairs. When Paul and Rapper passed, Paul winced as the warm breath of the dragon hit his back. For a split second, Paul had to stop because he felt lightheaded. The feelings from early childhood of looking under his bed before he went to sleep haunted him. He was always sure that dragon was under his bed or in his closet, just waiting for him to fall asleep so he could eat Paul for a midnight snack.

No, Paul thought. He wasn't going to let those feelings rule him. They were lies Satan had fed him to make him afraid. It wasn't going to work. This time it would be the other way around. As the dragon slept, Paul would take back what had been stolen. Then everything would be set right. Paul pressed on. *God has not given me a spirit of fear,* he remembered 2 Timothy 1:7, *but of power and of love and of self-discipline.*

Paul and Rapper reached the staircase. As quietly as he could, Rapper started up the steps. It was several stories up, but if they could just keep quiet enough...

"HEH-HEH-HEH-HEH-HEH."

Deep, guttural laughter filled the room. Paul closed his eyes. It couldn't be happening. Not now. Not like this. Not with the only exit on the *other* side of the room…on the *other* side of the dragon.

"HEH-HEH-HEH-HEH-HEH."

Paul and Rapper didn't move a muscle. From the corner of his eye, Paul could almost see Alex gulp from behind the dragon.

Slowly, as Paul and Rapper turned to face their enemy, the dragon arose. His cat-like, red eyes glared at the Superkids without blinking, as he stood to his feet. A slow, contemptuous smirk slid to the side of the dragon's mouth. As his webbed wings rippled, his scaly lips parted and sharp, milky teeth appeared in a smile.

Paul gulped. *I think he's closer to the size of* three *elephants,* Paul thought.

"WELCOME TO MY ABODE. WHAT A PLEASANT SURPRISE. THOU ART JUST IN TIME FOR DINNER…."

Behind the dragon, Alex didn't lose a beat. He scurried across the computer panels, looking for the shut-off switch. His foot hit one of the units.

Clink!

Like a snake ready to strike, Scratch whirled his head around and focused on Alex, who screamed with surprise.

"AN APPETIZER," the dragon taunted.

Bing! The dragon's claws popped out of his left paw's fingers like a handful of serrated knives. Alex's eyes grew wide.

Paul thought fast. Running down the steps, he slid around to the back of the dragon, who was now facing Alex.

"If you want him, you'll have to come through me!" Paul cried. He had heard that line before in a movie. And it worked. Too well.

Scratch spun around with that evil smile on his face. He

seemed to be enjoying the game. But Paul was going to do his best to make Scratch the loser. Boldly, he reached for his sword.

His hand grabbed air.

Paul looked down in surprise. His sword was gone! He had lost it in the river! How could he have forgotten *that* little piece of crucial information?!

Clank! Clank! Clank! Clank! Clank!

From halfway up the stairs, Rapper spied Paul's dilemma and reacted. Hitting the rail with his sword, he vied for the dragon's attention.

"Over here, Cinder Breath!" Rapper cried in a desperate rap, "Gimme whatever you got left!"

Scratch peered up at him, narrowing his reptilian eyes.

With a snap, Scratch unfurled his black wings in fury. They stretched through the lair like a gigantic canopy, blocking the light above. He shot a column of fire at Rapper, who ran up the stairs just in time to avoid a direct hit. The flames charred the brick wall.

Scratch's next blow came as he leapt into the air, supported by his wings, and came down on the stairway. Again, Rapper missed the blow, but the stairway suffered a direct hit. A section of the rock steps between the floor and Rapper crumbled away under the dragon's weight. Rapper wielded his sword, waiting for the dragon to come straight at him.

"Just go get Commander Kellie!" Paul shouted to Rapper, his voice echoing over the walls.

"But I'm better with a sword!" Rapper protested. "I should face the dragon!"

"*I* can't get up there now!" Paul shouted, pointing to the crumbled space in the stairs. Rapper considered Paul's point and then took off up the stairs.

Whooooosssshhhhh!

Paul saw Rapper's sword coming at him, end over end. In a full run, the Superkid had thrown it down so Paul could defend himself. The dragon followed the sword's movement and leapt forward to grab it when it clanked against the ground.

Paul dove and reached it first, rolling out of the way of the sharp claws. The dragon made a deep scratch in the ground right where Paul had been. Paul jumped up with sword in hand and waved it in front of Scratch. The beast roared and Paul tightened his grip on the sword.

Paul glanced at Rapper. He was running up the stairs, two at a time. Paul couldn't see Alex.

Against all odds, Paul ran forward and sliced the sword at the dragon's leg. As it hit its mark, the dragon roared again in anger, throwing fire into the air. Paul struck again in the same place, going for the greatest weakness, and hit with all his might.

The force of the hit, matched with a sudden kick by Scratch, knocked the sword out of Paul's grip. It hurtled through the air. Paul raced to catch it, but Scratch's bony fingers caught it first. The dragon peered down at Paul and pulled the sword back for a strong blow.

Pitching the sword at Paul, the dragon screamed with delight. Paul dodged the sword in a dive. It wedged itself into a crack of mortar in the wall. Paul jumped up to get it.

He couldn't reach it. It was lodged too high.

"HEH-HEH-HEH-HEH-HEH."

On the other side of Scratch, Paul could see Alex scrambling. His friend was digging away at some rocks in the wall.

"THOU HAST NO CHANCE AGAINST ME," the dragon

threatened. "THOU ART SMALL."

Paul thought of his name—that's what it meant. "Size doesn't matter," Paul argued. "The Scriptures say in Matthew 17:20 that if I have faith even as small as a mustard seed, it's big enough to move a mountain like you!"

Alex kept removing rocks.

"NO!!!" Scratch bellowed. "I HAVE ALL KNOWL-EDGE!!! THE SCRIPTURES OF WHICH THOU SPEAK-EST EXIST NOT!! NOTHING IS UNKNOWN TO ME!!!"

"Your pride is your downfall," Paul replied.

Scratch reared back and his nostrils flared. Paul heard a gur-gling sound as the dragon parted his lips, about to burn Paul to a crisp.

Alex threw his hand into the hole he created and pulled a switch.

POW!

The walls flickered. The ground flickered. Scratch flickered.

Like seeing through an X-ray machine, Paul saw the steel and wooden mechanics underneath the holo-projections. Scratch's steel skeleton glimmered beneath the fading holo-graphic image.

Scratch roared, bewildered.

Rapper broke through the holo-projection of the door at the top of the stairs and ran out with Commander Kellie.

The room buzzed and whirred. Scratch disappeared, leaving only an unmoving, steel skeleton in his place. The facade of the castle room faded away and wood and steel replaced it.

All was silent.

Paul's heartbeat slowed down as he took a breath of fresh air.

"I did it!" Alex cried. "I found the main switch and ended the program!"

"You're the man!" Rapper shouted from the top of a catwalk, pointing down at Alex.

"Way to go, Superkid!" Commander Kellie congratulated.

Fffffftttttt!

Ffffffftttttt!

Suddenly, to everyone's amazement, the black brick returned. The long stairs returned. The tall chamber returned. The scratched ground returned.

"HEH-HEH-HEH-HEH-HEH."

"A backup system!" Paul cried. "There has to be a back-up system!"

Alex scanned the computer panels. "I don't see one! It's not here!"

Rapper and Commander Kellie started down the stairs.

Alex pulled out the map once again. He slapped it on the computer panel and ran his hand across it.

"Everything leads to this central chamber!" Alex shouted. "It doesn't make sense!"

In a flash, Scratch returned, his dark, brownish-green scales appearing stronger than ever. The beast's red eyes focused on Paul. His head lowered until his eyes were across from Paul's, his vicious snout in Paul's face.

In his deep, guttural voice, Old Scratch proudly announced, "*I* AM THE BACKUP SYSTEM."

Paul's mouth dropped open as the dragon reared back and brought a claw to his own chest. He popped open a scale right over his heart. Behind the scale was an electronic panel with a hand-switch—the backup system—clearly "on." Scratch smiled, his milky teeth gleaming. He let the scale pop shut as he howled in delight.

Commander Kellie and Rapper stopped running as Scratch's tail whipped through the air near the stairs. Paul ran to the side, looking for any kind of advantage. His sword was down the river. Rapper's sword was two feet higher than he could reach. Alex's sword was—

Shhhhhhhhhhhhh!

Paul looked down to see Alex's sword coming at him, sliding across the floor. He grabbed it in a swift motion and waved it in the air. Scratch dropped down to the ground again on all fours, letting out a low growl.

Paul ran left, then right, trying to buy Alex and Rapper time to get out of the room. But they couldn't get past the dragon. Something told Paul that Scratch was just toying with them anyway. Paul refused to dwell on it. He thought about that make-believe dragon that had scared him so many times as a young child and he thought about this dragon that was working overtime to destroy him now.

With energy running through his body, Paul sprinted forward toward the dragon's legs and shoved the sword straight into the beast's kneecap.

Clink!

Paul looked down. The blade of his sword snapped in half upon striking Scratch.

Paul suddenly found it hard to breathe. He pulled back, throwing the handle and half blade to the side.

Paul stood there before the dragon, with no weapon in his hand, no idea in his head. Like it or not, the Superkids were back where they had started: on the verge of becoming a hologram's dinner.

Alex stood in the back, shaking his head. He didn't know what to do. Commander Kellie and Rapper stood on the stairs in prayer.

Like a mammoth school bully, Scratch looked down at Paul and laughed. And laughed. And laughed. He knew he was clearly the victor.

Once again, the pompous dragon leaned down to Paul, his snout in Paul's face, his fiery eyes glowing.

"WHAT SAYEST THOU FOR THYSELF, BOY?" he asked.

Paul felt like the dragon had stabbed him. He was proving his superiority to Paul. He was taunting him. He was winning.

"I'm weaponless," Paul admitted, not taking his eyes off the dragon's.

Scratch's reptilian eyebrows narrowed as he leaned farther into Paul's face.

"TELL ME SOMETHING I KNOW NOT."

As a sudden surge of inspiration, the Holy Spirit poured His wisdom into Paul's spirit. Paul narrowed his eyebrows, still staring ahead.

Paul leaned into the dragon until he was as close as he could get without letting his nose touch the filthy beast. Then he said, "All right. I *will* tell you something you don't know."

Paul reached into his back pocket without even a blink and pulled out the sword he'd almost forgotten he had. It was the *other* sword he had been training with all week. It was the Sword he knew best.

Paul shoved it up in front of Scratch's right eye and quoted Hebrews 4:12.

"The Word of God is living and active," he said coolly. "It's sharper than any double-edged sword."

"WHERE DIDST THOU GET THAT?!"

"It's the Word of God," Paul stated. "Isaiah 55:11—It never returns to me empty, but it accomplishes what God desires and achieves the purpose for which He sent it."

"'TIS A LIE!! IT DOTH NOT EXIST!!"

"John 1:1—In the beginning was the Word, and the Word

was with God, and the Word was God. And it became flesh and lived among us!"

"NO!!!" Scratch reared up and threw his clawed, front paws in the air. His black wings unfurled and flapped. "THOU CANST DEFEAT ME NOT!"

"Second Corinthians 10:4—The weapons we fight with are not the weapons of the world. No—ours have divine power to demolish strongholds!"

The dragon turned away from Paul in absolute disgust and turned his attention to Commander Kellie and Rapper. As he reared back to bathe them with fire, Commander Kellie and Rapper cried out Isaiah 54:17. "No weapon forged against us will prevail!"

At once, the dragon threw his head up in fury and the column of fire shot straight up, to no avail, bursting out of the castle.

From behind him, Alex shouted John 10:28. "We shall never perish! No one can snatch us out of God's hand!"

Scratch took a large step back, bombarded by the power of the Word. He scratched the walls in a blind tantrum.

Full of boldness from the Holy Spirit, Paul dodged a wild strike from Scratch's claws and ran *underneath* the dragon. He dodged the beast's foot and grabbed at the scale over his heart. Scratch screamed when Paul opened it and Paul lost his grip. It slammed shut again.

Scratch tried to take flight, but was too infuriated to get his wings to carry him. They flapped in the air as he blew fire and smoke around the room haphazardly.

Paul leapt up again, this time with his Bible in hand. When he popped open the panel, Paul jammed his Bible between the hinges, jarring the scale open.

With the Word of God lodged in his heart, the dragon—dead set against it—couldn't even concentrate. It was exactly the advantage Paul needed.

The Superkid reached in, grabbed the lever to the backup system and pulled it into the "off" position with all his might.

"NOOOOOOOOOOOOOOO!!!"

Scratch flickered.

Paul shoved the backup system back to "on."

Scratch flashed on.

Paul shoved it off again.

Then on again.

Then off again.

Then on again.

Then off again.

KA-POW! BOOOOOMMM!!!

Scratch roared and cried out in absolute fury as the system overloaded, starting in his chest.

As Scratch flashed into oblivion, a column of fire billowed out of his steel skeleton and shot into the sky. With the system going haywire, the ceiling of the holoworld burst into flames.

Paul grabbed his Bible out of what now looked like nothing more than a cracking, steel skeleton. Alex rushed forward and met Paul. Commander Kellie and Rapper raced down the remainder of the stairs, leaping over the area of steps Scratch had ripped away.

When Paul saw Commander Kellie coming toward him, entirely free, it was all he could do to keep from letting out the tears. But there was no time now. Paul gave his commander a quick hug.

"Thank you, Paul," she whispered to her student and friend.

"I'm so sorry," Paul whispered back.

"Paul, it's over now, it's over," Commander Kellie returned.

Paul, Commander Kellie, Rapper and Alex all suddenly stumbled. The ground began shifting, rumbling. Scratch's old skeleton snapped and collapsed, crashing to the ground. Paul looked up and saw the burning sky above. The room began to quake.

"It's not over yet!" Paul proclaimed.

"What's happening?!" cried Rapper. "I thought the system was going to shut down and disappear!"

"It's overloaded!" Alex exclaimed. "There's too much

power surging through the circuits! It's gonna blow!"

"We have to get out of here!" Rapper shouted.

"How far away is the exit?" Commander Kellie cried.

Alex held up the map. "We came in at the *end* of the river! It's a long way!"

Paul turned to Commander Kellie for direction. She was the commander, after all. She locked eyes with Paul, confidence written all over her face.

"Paul, you're in charge," she said.

Paul's eyes gleamed. There was no question in Paul's mind that she still believed in him. Paul nodded. "You think that river is still flowing fast?" he asked Alex. Alex shrugged. Paul said, "Let's find out!"

Paul took off out the side door and hit the spiraling stairway at top speed. Commander Kellie, Rapper and Alex didn't waste any time keeping up.

One flight, two flights, three flights they ran up.

The walls spurted dust as the bricks cracked and mortar ripped.

Four flights, five flights, six flights, around and around.

The stairs rumbled and started dropping through. Paul leapt. Commander Kellie leapt. Rapper leapt. Alex leapt.

Seven flights and the stairs dead ended.

"It closed!" Paul cried. "Find the switch that opens it! Find it!"

The bricks continued to crack and crumble as the Superkids pressed one brick after another.

A grinding sound filled the hallway.

"Got it!" Alex announced, pressing his foot on the corner brick of a stair. The ceiling door pulled back and the crew of adventurers spilled out. Paul led them quickly through the round hall to the exit door.

BAM! Paul slammed open the door with his shoulder and burst outside. The sunlight mixed with the burning sky made Paul's eyes ache. But there was no time to stop. They ran straight out to the river, trying to run steadily on the shaking ground. When they reached the river, they all came to a sudden halt.

The river was no longer simply rolling downstream. It was a torrent now, a white-water rapids. Paul scanned the shore. There!

Paul ran to a large log.

"We'll have to ride this down!" Paul cried.

Ka-BOOOOOOOOMMMMMMMMMMMMM!!!

Commander Kellie and the Superkids jumped as the dark castle behind them imploded with a thunderous, rumbling crash. For a short moment, they were stunned. They had barely made it out in time.

"How are we going to ride a log?!" Rapper questioned.

"We'll just have to hang on!" Commander Kellie said as more of an order than a suggestion. "I don't think this place is going to last much longer!"

The overloaded holoworld was becoming increasingly unstable.

Paul, Commander Kellie, Rapper and Alex raised the log together and—on the count of three—dashed straight into the torrential rapids.

SPLAAASHHHHHHHHHH!

The four adventurers, pulled by the weight of the log and the current, shot forward so fast they could barely keep their eyes open.

Paul held on tight, his arms aching and begging to let go, but like the others, he resisted. As they rushed downriver, water surged into their faces, threatening to drown them.

THUMP! It seemed like forever until the log finally smashed into a riverbank, throwing the team head-over-heels onto shore.

"This is it!" Alex shouted, getting up. "This is the end! The holoworld doesn't stretch beyond this point!"

"We're back at the beginning?!" Rapper yelled.

"Yes!" Alex called back. "This is where we came in!"

"Where is it?!" Commander Kellie cried, standing with the others. "Where's the door?!"

Paul looked around. He couldn't see it. He couldn't even tell which way was north.

Crash! Boom!

Trees came down around them, falling like toothpicks. Fireballs shot down from the sky, igniting the ground in flames.

"We have to get out!" Alex warned.

Szzzzzzzzzzzz!

For a split-second, the holoworld reverted back to its steel and mechanics. The trees looked like girders and the ground like cement. Fire spread. Then it was back to the medieval, burning environment again.

"I saw it!" Commander Kellie announced, pointing behind them. "It's right there!"

Alex ran forward and felt around for a door handle. He tightened his fist around an oddly flattened tree branch.

"Got it!" Alex shouted. He pulled.

Nothing.

He pushed. Nothing.

"It's locked!"

"Locked?!!!" Paul couldn't believe it.

BAM! A fiery tree crashed down beside him. Paul jumped back. The shaking earth pulled him to his knees.

Paul threw his arms around a fallen tree trunk before him.

"You have an idea?!" Commander Kellie shouted.

"We'll ram it!" Paul answered.

Commander Kellie, Rapper and Alex grabbed hold of the tree, too, angling it at the door. Rapper, on the far end, shrieked. "It's on fire!"

"Better it than us!" Paul shouted back. "One! Two! Three!"

SMASH!

Commander Kellie and the Superkids charged forward, ramming the tree trunk into the invisible wall, right where the commander had seen the door.

"Again!" Commander Kellie ordered.

SMASH!

SMASH!

BOOM!

The door crumpled under the force, bursting open. Commander Kellie and her rescuing knights dropped the trunk in an instant. At once, all four shot out the door like bullets out of a gun.

The cement steps and city street outside were an odd contrast to the medieval environment from which they came, but were a welcome sight nonetheless.

Taking the stairs three at a time, they rushed away from the building and across the street, reaching cover just in time to turn around and watch the building behind them explode.

FA-TOOOOOOOOOOOOOOOOMMMMMMMMMMMM!!!

Steel, fire, ash, wood and concrete flew everywhere as a gigantic ball of fire unfolded into the sky. Black smoke spread from the crumbling building, turning the sunny day into sudden dusk.

Paul heard sirens in the distance.

✪ ✪ ✪

"In a major setback for social renewal, NME's forthcoming 'holo-jail' ended in catastrophe today. The pile of ash and bricks behind me is all that's left of the holo-jail test site. NME sources tell us this action is the result of a right-wing terrorist 'joke'—one that left none of the NME officials laughing. NME is planning a thorough investigation into the matter, saying they are 'sick and tired of being held captive by terrorist actions.' This is Bab Tidings for NME-TV News."

"TV off," Paul ordered. The television clicked off. "Would you get a load of that?" Paul said, nodding toward the television set.

Paul, Rapper and Alex lay on their beds, taking a long, relaxing breather from their whirlwind adventure.

Paul and Rapper shared a bunk bed. Rapper was on the top bunk, Paul on the bottom. Alex was catty-corner to them, on the top bunk of his bed, with a computer terminal built underneath.

With the television now off, all three Superkids stared at the ceiling.

"'NME sources,'" Rapper said with a smirk. "Sounds like Dread made it out all right."

"Yep," Alex agreed, numbly.

The three Superkids stayed silent for about 15 minutes, just thinking.

"You know, though," Paul said finally, "I slayed that dragon."

"Yep," Alex agreed again.

Rapper smiled. "Thank God, I'll never have to face a dragon again."

Paul nodded, thoughtfully. "I know I won't either."

The door to room 312 slid open and Commander Kellie entered. She was dressed in a fresh, clean, royal-blue commander's outfit. Three gold stripes were on her sleeves, three gold stars on each side of her collar. Her straight brown hair curled under at her shoulders.

"Hey guys, just wanted to remind you that tomorrow we're back to regular activities," she announced to the three young men. "See you at 0600 hours?"

Paul nodded. "Yes, Commander."

Commander Kellie turned to leave, but stopped midway. She rubbed the back of her neck with her hand. "Are you three as tired as I am?"

Paul chuckled. "We're exhausted."

The commander caught each of the Superkid's eyes and then softly said, "Thank you again, Superkids. What you did was very brave. Each time I prayed, I was confident in knowing you wouldn't give up—no matter what the enemy threw at you."

"Well," Paul said with a smile, "hopefully you won't ever be in a position like that again. I'm through setting forests on fire."

From the top bunk, Rapper spoke up. "...and villages, and castles, and...."

"Thanks, Rapper, we get the picture," Paul said.

"Don't forget buildings," Alex piped. "He blew up a building."

Paul flipped over on his bed. "I did not. It wasn't totally me that—" Paul covered his head with his pillow as his friends laughed with him.

"Well, anyway," Commander Kellie said, "I appreciate

your help. You all did an extraordinary job—as Superkids *and* as friends."

"It was God and His Word in us," Paul pointed out.

Commander Kellie smiled. "I know." She turned and walked out the door. Before closing it behind her, she turned and said with a wink, "Let's make that wake-up call for 0800 hours instead." Then she exited.

Paul, Rapper and Alex stayed silent for most of the evening's remainder. They lay and thought, and let their bruises heal. And Paul felt good. Yes, he started off on the wrong foot, but he ended up with the victory. With his team—his friends—he had rescued his commander and defeated a dragon.

As Paul's eyelids fell heavy, he let out a long, relaxing breath. As a young man growing up in the Academy, his day's work was complete. And as a Superkid, he knew this adventure wouldn't be his last.

Prayer for Salvation

Father God, I believe that Jesus is Your Son and that You raised Him from the dead for me. Jesus, I give my life to You. Right now, I make You the Lord of my life and choose to follow You forever. I love You and I know You love me. Thank You, Jesus, for giving me a new life. Thank You for coming into my heart and being my Savior. I am a child of God! Amen.

About the Author

For more than 10 years, **Christopher P. N. Maselli** has been sharing God's Word with kids through fiction. He is the author of more than 30 books including Zonderkidz' *Laptop* series and the *Superkids* Adventures. He is also the founder of TruthPop.com, dedicated to reaching 'tweens with the Truth through pop culture.

A graduate of Oral Roberts University, Chris lives in Fort Worth, Texas, with his wife, Gena. He is actively involved in his church's *KIDS Church* program, and his hobbies include inline skating, collecting *It's a Wonderful Life* movie memorabilia and "way too much" computing.

World Offices
of Kenneth Copeland Ministries

For more information about KCM and a free
catalog, please write the office nearest you:

Kenneth Copeland Ministries
Fort Worth, Texas 76192-0001

Kenneth Copeland
Locked Bag 2600
Mansfield Delivery Centre
QUEENSLAND 4122
AUSTRALIA

Kenneth Copeland
Post Office Box 15
BATH
BA1 3XN
U.K.

Kenneth Copeland
Private Bag X 909
FONTAINEBLEAU
2032
REPUBLIC OF
SOUTH AFRICA

Kenneth Copeland
PO Box 3111 STN LCD 1
Langley BC
V3A 4R3
CANADA

Kenneth Copeland Ministries
Post Office Box 84
L'VIV 79000
UKRAINE

We're Here for You!

Believer's Voice of Victory **Television Broadcast**

Join Kenneth and Gloria Copeland and the *Believer's Voice of Victory* broadcasts Monday through Friday and on Sunday each week, and learn how faith in God's Word can take your life from ordinary to extraordinary. This teaching from God's Word is designed to get you where you want to be—*on top!*

You can catch the *Believer's Voice of Victory* broadcast on your local, cable or satellite channels.

Check your local listings for times and stations in your area.

Believer's Voice of Victory **Magazine**

Enjoy inspired teaching and encouragement from Kenneth and Gloria Copeland and guest ministers each month in the *Believer's Voice of Victory* magazine. Also included are real-life testimonies of God's miraculous power and divine intervention in the lives of people just like you!

It's more than just a magazine—it's a ministry.

To receive a FREE subscription to *Believer's Voice of Victory,* write to:

Kenneth Copeland Ministries
Fort Worth, Texas 76192-0001
Or call:
(800) 600-7395
(7 a.m.-5 p.m. CT)
Or visit our Web site at:
www.kcm.org

If you are writing from outside the U.S., please contact the KCM office nearest you. Addresses for all Kenneth Copeland Ministries offices are listed on the previous pages.